MY CAPTAINS

Memoirs of a Scottish West Coast fisherman

Tom Ralston

SCOTTISH CULTURAL PRESS

First published 1995
Scottish Cultural Press
PO Box 106
Aberdeen AB9 8ZE
Tel: 01224 583777/ Fax: 01224 575337

British Library Cataloguing in Publication Data
A catalogue record for this book is available
from the British Library

ISBN: 1 898218 27 7

Also from Scottish Cultural Press:

MORAY FIRTH SHIPS AND TRADE during the nineteenth century
Ian Hustwick

Printed by
BPC-AUP Ltd, Aberdeen, Scotland

PREFACE

Come with me on a look back in time, and be introduced to some of the remarkable characters I have met during my career on the west coast of Scotland, firstly as a fisherman, then later as a Lifeboat coxswain, and fish buyer.

In our explorations we travel from the Outer Hebrides to the Isle of Man, and then east to Whitby, but the bulk of my stories are from the west coast of Scotland in general, Mallaig and the Clyde in particular.

As this is not an autobiography, I was for some time puzzled as to how to link together the random memories of a lifetime spent among the pioneering giants of the fishing profession, until Angus Martin – my cousin – sent me a copy of his poem, part of which is reproduced below. This poem, the most evocative I have ever read, led me to visualise these men – or their spirits – gathered together around the ghostly fireside of Angus's dream. What a gathering that would be!

Receiving the captains into my home
required no preparations; they came
with the gait of men accustomed
to straddling water on the thin
comfort of drunken planking,
and rolled themselves politely through the door.
There was whisky for one hand and cake
for the other, and a window beyond
the clockface and the hanging light,
and they gathered there before the glass
seeing themselves reflected, and remembering
the outer space of wind and sea.

Let me shake your hands. Goodbye, captains.
Be careful out there, where you are bound.
Perhaps you have forgotten certain dangers –
fingers of gloomy shore and the sunken teeth of reefs –
and remember there are new lights everywhere.
You'll manage, I dare say, but do not tell me where
you're going, or I may wish to go with you,
a passenger just – no skills to serve you with –
sitting below, hearing the tongues of the sea
and the creaking of the skiff 's old bones,
a boy in the bilgy dark, hunched at a mug of tea,
far from home, my captains, very far from home.

The poem also gave me the title for this book, and for this, and for all his help and encouragement, I will be forever in Angus's debt.

It is not my wish or my intention to hurt the feelings of anyone alive, nor to harm the reputation of those who are now dead.

Tom Ralston
Lundin Links
January 1995

ACKNOWLEDGEMENTS

I would like to acknowledge the advice, encouragement, and criticisms freely given by my cousin Angus Martin of Campbeltown, who not only supplied several of the photographs used, but also allowed me to quote from part of his wonderful poem. Without him, I doubt if this book would ever have been written. Thanks to the lovely Sue Hughan – an immensely talented artist from Kellas – for her superb line drawings; thanks to Aberdeen Journals for permission to use their photograph of 'Dodie' Alexander and Albert Watt; to Matt Sloan and Grieve Gemmell for their photographs; and finally grateful thanks to my friend Bill Flett of Anstruther, for allowing me access to his unique collection of priceless photographs.

This book is dedicated
to the memories of those who appear in it,
and around whose lives it is crafted.

1

Gayfield Place was a good community to be born into. In 1935 there were over one hundred people living in the three-storey-high grey tenement on the north-western extremity of Dalintober – once a fishing village in its own right but now considered by most as a part of Campbeltown. Subsequently demolished and the site still lying undeveloped, Gayfield then glared at the town as defiantly as it faced the all too frequent south-westerly gales.

I was only four years old when the Second World War started.

I have no memory of the beginning of this insanity, and the fact that it deprived me of my father's company almost from the outset, was not of any great importance to me at that time. His early Naval postings – firstly to Milford Haven, and later to Lamlash on Arran – meant that my mother and I, of choice, joined him at these places for over a year in total. There is also a probability that the war against Hitler was indirectly responsible for the fact that there is a six year gap between my brother and myself, an age difference which meant that we were not as close as we might otherwise have been – a source of much regret to me, and no doubt to him also. I remember very little of Milford Haven, but I do remember a little of the time spent on Arran, although I was still very young.

My father was Coxswain on the *Silver Grey* which, in civilian life, had been a ring-net fishing boat in Campbeltown, referred to in knowing circles as a 'ringer', but which had been commandeered on to the Admiralty list as the *R3*, and was now rather optimistically referred to as an inshore patrol boat.

Their task was to monitor the anti-submarine booms which had been laid across the entrances to Lamlash Bay. This duty was carried out with diligence for some time, but when it became apparent that this was not some death or glory mission, but rather a long, drawn out, boring routine with little chance of the action they then craved, the crew – who were all ex-fishermen – convinced the Lieutenant in charge of this diminutive warship that they could combine their patrolling duties with a little bit of trawling. After all, they argued, they should do their bit to help feed the hungry. That they used the money earned from selling the catch to augment their meagre Naval pay, was of no consequence of course!

I believe that these fishermen were also responsible for brainwashing the officers in command at Lamlash into believing that they should have a test firing of one of the two depth-charges which were (more in hope than in anger I am certain) mounted on the stern of the boats.

This test was conducted off the Cock of Arran where the water was considered deep enough to safely detonate the charge, which was adjusted to its deepest setting for the occasion. The corpses of the fish which were the only result of this experiment, were gleefully gathered in and sold, the amount being added to the week's beer money!

I distinctly remember being afraid of 'funny noises' during the night, and being shown where they originated from – a sink full of plaice, still flapping around, which took a long time in dying.

I often heard repeated the story of how a dead rat had been put into the seaboot belonging to one of the crew, a very excitable man who had been christened James Robertson, but who rejoiced in the nickname 'Gipsy'. This was done one night just before the gullible Gipsy was called for watch. When he drowsily pulled on his boot, and then grumpily shook it to remove the obstruction which his foot had encountered, the drowsiness and grumpiness were forgotten as he battered the remains of the poor beast around the cabin, bellowing like a bull as he attempted to 'kill' the offending corpse!

I had always thought this was a lovely story, but could not swallow the part of it which alleged that poor Gipsy thought that he had in fact been successful in killing this rodent. I was, therefore, completely amazed to find a photograph in the Scottish Fisheries Museum at Anstruther in May 1994, of Gipsy on the foredeck of the *R3*, proudly holding his prize by the tail!

'Gipsy' Robertson

It was in Lamlash, too, that my long-suffering mother had one of the worst experiences of her life to date. I had gone down the pier to see if my father was around, and had succeeded in falling into the water. An alert sailor recovered me, none the worse for my ducking, but my companions – most of whom were much older than I – insisted on wheeling me homeward in a wheelbarrow. One of them was sent ahead on his bicycle to warn my mother that her offspring was being taken home, and that he was wet.

This messenger rounded the corner below the house we were renting, saw my mother sitting outside knitting in the sunshine and called –'Tommy fell into the water. They're bringing him home in a wheelbarrow!' – then shot off back to the rest of the gang, leaving her completely distraught as she awaited the arrival of the 'corpse' of her son !

Returning with my mother from our visits to Milford Haven and Arran, I spent the rest of the war years back in Campbeltown in the safe haven that was Gayfield, whilst my father was serving abroad.

Campbeltown is built around the head of a beautiful horseshoe-shaped loch which is almost landlocked. Access to the open sea is gained via the narrow channel to the north side of the island of Davaar.

Davaar is only a part-time island, being easily accessible dry shod across the shingle isthmus called the Dhorlin, for around half of the tidal period. The loch is sheltered on the north and the south sides by high hills – a gap to the west leads to Machrihanish, a sandy plain which still houses an important military airfield. This harbour, on the east side of the peninsula of Kintyre, was ideally situated to shelter the Naval units delegated to guard the entrance to the Firth of Clyde in time of war. The town had reached the peaks of prosperity in the early nineteenth century when it supported – in addition to its farming, shipbuilding, and fishing communities – some thirty or so distilleries and all their allied trades. A coal mine at Machrihanish five miles from the town was the catalyst for the construction of a rail link between it and the pier in Campbeltown. At the time of my birth, however, the coal mine had closed, the railway had been scrapped, the number of working distilleries had shrunk to two, and the shipbuilding yard at Trench Point had also ceased trading.

My war memories are, of course, good ones. It has become obvious to me, with many others, that the mind kindly deletes most of the bad things, to the great benefit of the good ones, so that the air raids – fortunately few – are imprinted upon my mind as times when I was forced to hide under the table of a downstairs neighbour, and was annoyed at not being allowed to watch all the pretty lights. The knowledge, gained in the light of the morning following one such raid, that the Royal Hotel had been hit and that a number of fatalities had resulted – including a party of Wrens – meant only that I was annoyed at not being allowed to view the damage.

Sea mines dropped from enemy aircraft and meant for the loch, but in fact hitting and destroying several houses at Trench Point, meant the loss of one of

3

the best friends that the Clyde fishermen ever had, Archibald Stewart, a prominent lawyer in the town. At the time however, this was only another source of excitement to me. Sadness is an emotion which I think is either fleeting or is totally absent in the young, whose interests are usually completely self-centred. It is worthwhile noting that Archibald Stewart was buried in Kilkerran graveyard on the south side of Campbeltown Loch, and that he was given what is to me the most impressive headstone in the cemetery. It is not large – in fact it is quite small. It is not the most expensive. It was however erected, with the permission of his family, by the Tarbert fishermen – 'In memory of a true friend'. Surely a tremendous compliment to a man who was legal adviser to them, and to all of the Clyde fishing community for many years.

Gayfield Place was also a good place in which to spend one's formative years.

There was a strong community spirit there, fostered no doubt by the lack of material wealth, coupled with the need to stick together in what were difficult times. I fondly remember the all-too-few occasions when the tenants of this building got together and hired a bus, which took us to picnic on one of the many beaches of Kintyre. Only a few buses were available for hire, and those most in demand had plush-covered, sprung seats. However, there was a so-called 'utility' model, which differed from the others in that it had wooden seats. Such is the perverseness, or thrawnness, of youth, that I well remember hoping that we got the 'utility' model, so that I could relish the scorn heaped by the hirers upon the head of the hapless driver, who of course had no choice in deciding which vehicle was sent to pick us up.

There was no television of course, and radio reception was subject to the vagaries of a generally unreliable accumulator to power the equally unreliable radio receiver, yet we never seemed to be bored. Going to the cinema was dependent mainly upon one's skill at collecting jam jars or lemonade bottles, which were turned into ready cash at one of the many shops which offered payment for the returned containers. The oft-experienced dearth of jam jars, and therefore of money, meant that the cinema was a rare treat which, with hindsight, was no real hardship.

Indeed, it occurs to me now that viewing one of the then popular films such as *The Three Musketeers*, or *Zorro*, was followed by the frantic fashioning of wooden swords with which we re-enacted the fight scenes we had just witnessed. 'Roy Rogers' films meant that for days we rode imaginary horses every-where, shooting at everything which moved, with our hand-carved carbines. This fact is at odds with today's purveyors of excessive violence and filth, who produce 'experts' to prove that we are not influenced by what we view. There were then two cinemas in the town; only one now remains, and it is a part-time Bingo hall.

The darker nights brought on the games which seem largely forgotten now: 'aleevo', 'kick the can', 'tig' and the like. They kept us running, hiding, and arguing all evening, and it was only the dreaded call from mother which took us very reluctantly to the zinc bath by the gaslight in front of the coal fire, then upstairs to bed. I do not recall ever finishing any of these games. Perhaps they are still running somewhere?

Our mothers were fortunate too in that there was never, I am certain, any need for them to worry about us being abused in any way. Such monstrosities are a product of the civil liberties which we now all enjoy. I am equally sure however, that they found other things to worry about. There was for instance, a long spell when adults spoke in hushed tones of 'the ghost', which tales we children were not supposed to hear. There was always someone who had heard of another sighting, but I am sure that this white-clad figure – who never harmed anyone to my knowledge – existed only in the fertile imagination of a few gossips, who had found a new way to command the attention upon which they thrived.

Apart from the aforementioned air raids, there was one other wartime occasion which engendered great excitement among the youth in the town – the 'Commando raid'. This was a simulated invasion of the town by Commandos, which was to be opposed by the local Home Guard, whose members of course were all well known to us. One of the Gayfield boys, Arthur MacMillan, gained great kudos from the fact that his father was not only in the Home Guard, but was a wireless operator, and as such carried a most imposing radio upon his back.

On the day of the 'invasion', several of us were scouting the hills around the town looking for our new-found heroes, the Commandos, when we chanced upon a well-concealed troop of Home Guards waiting in ambush, complete with radio operator who immediately told us all in general, and his son in particular, to 'Clear Off', in no uncertain terms. This we did, and of course, when we soon afterwards found our Commandos, we took great delight in guiding them to the Home Guards' hiding place. I am led to believe that Arthur's father made a remarkable recovery after being killed by the Commandos, and made a valiant attempt to inflict the same punishment upon poor Arthur!

In Gayfield Place there lived the first of my potential 'Captains'.

Donald Brown occupied a room and kitchen on the right hand side of the main entrance close. This was a bad place to live, as it was vulnerable to the oft-times played prank of tying the door handle to the one opposite, then retiring to a safe distance to view the result of knocking on both doors!

Donald, or 'Brown' as he was commonly called, hailed originally from Carradale, a village some fifteen miles to the north of Campbeltown, and where in his earlier days he had been a fisherman. He was a big soft-spoken man, inclined to stoutness, and fortunately for us he was like most large men, very easy-going and good-natured. To the despair of the ladies who – because their husbands were away in one or other of the Services – made up the bulk of his neighbours, he kept ferrets in his coal cellar. Needless to say, he was not married.

One of my earliest recollections of Brown was the day his chimney caught fire. This caused a great commotion among the rest of the tenants, some of whom had washing hanging out to dry directly in line with the soot which fell as a result of the fire. Brown denied all knowledge of this conflagration, despite the fact that his face was blackened, and that his house – seen through the tiny crack which was all that he would allow the door to be opened – was redolent of sooty fumes. As a result of this fire, the MacBrayne brothers, who were great friends to Brown, prevailed upon him to get his chimney cleaned, and engaged one of the Foster brothers to do the job.

Now the Fosters were well-known to us all, having the alleged habit of using a bicycle to ride the length of the hall, when anyone knocked on their door. It was a matter of some honour that the caller should protest that whichever brother answered the door was not the required one, which resulted in this poor man having to turn the cycle around, pedal back down the fifteen feet of hallway, and then the whole hilarious process would start all over again with the 'correct' brother!

The great day dawned. Davie Foster arrived with his rods strapped to his bicycle, and work commenced. Since Brown was on the ground floor of the three-storey building, a lot of rods would be required to be screwed together to enable the brush to reach the top of the chimney – a time-consuming job. Brown, an acknowledged expert at delegating work, deployed Cecil Finn (another contemporary of mine in Gayfield, who is now President of the Scottish Fishermen's Federation) and me to stand across the road from the front of the building to watch keenly for the first sign of the brush appearing from the chimney can, and to report this sighting to him in the house where he was doing that which he was by nature best suited for – supervising the work. Of course the already limited attention span of two young lads is a tiny fraction of that of one young lad, so the first sign we had that all was not well was when there arose from the rear of the building a great and increasing uproar.

It appears that while our attention was diverted, the brush had emerged from the top of the chimney and had bent – of course backward away from us – towards the rear of the building, and was currently showering soot freely on to the washing lines which were full of what had previously been nice clean washing!

When peace had been, if not restored then at least contemplated, Davie announced that as a result of the severe bend in the cane caused by the weight of the brush pulling it down over the chimney can, he could not now retrieve it by the normal method of pulling it back down the chimney. A noisy meeting was convened in the backyard before someone produced a ladder, with which assistance Davie climbed from the top landing of the building on to the roof, followed by loud and conflicting advice from the by now thoroughly agitated ladies. Once safely at the chimney head, he took off the brush, allowing Brown to withdraw the freed canes back into the house.

Davie, safely back on terra firma, then declared himself not to be satisfied with the job, so he clambered back up on to the roof bearing a heavy metal sphere which was designed to take the brush, suspended on a rope, down the uncleaned chimney. He chose the wrong one!

When this ball, accompanied by the brush arrived at some speed – unannounced, but accompanied by a great cloud of free-flying soot – into the kitchen of the house directly above Brown's (which was occupied by the diminutive but vociferous Willie MacAulay, better known as 'Cala', and his sister), the resulting discussion filled in any missing words in our budding vocabularies, and has provided mirth on many occasions since.

Halcyon days indeed.

Brown provided a happy shelter to us on many occasions, and his harmless tales of his time as a fisherman whetted our appetite for the life and taught us a lot about the sea. He taught us how to mend nets, and it was a matter of some pride to me and to Cecil no doubt that we were reasonably proficient in this sphere when at last the time came for us to leave school and start our working lives as apprentice fishermen. Brown never told a malicious tale about anyone, and one of his instructions was never to be without a knife: 'It might save your life boy if you get a rope wrapped around your leg and it is pulling you into the water.' Although thankfully this never happened, I still heed his sound advice. This small pocket knife, the only tool which a fisherman was expected to carry, is still so important to me that my wife has, on more than one occasion, taken it to me when I inadvertently left it at home.

A Captain? Well, perhaps not quite. My Captains do not easily attain that rank, but a great character nonetheless, and one who should not be forgotten.

It would not do to leave school and to embark upon serious life without mentioning some of the long-suffering teachers who tried to instil some degree of learning into our largely unresponsive minds.

In Mr Banks – 'Kubla Khan' to us all – I recognise, too late, a man who had a great love for the English language, and who must have despaired of us ever grasping its rudiments. 'Big Bob' Graham tried to teach us the delicacies of French – with a kind word to boys who struggled with English. I now express to them the debt which should have been acknowledged while they were alive.

No mention of Campbeltown Grammar School would be complete however without a word about 'Wee Mickey', as we knew Malcolm G MacCallum, the music teacher.

He was, as his nickname might convey, a small man with a florid complexion who wore a small bristling moustache. His temper was legendary, and I will never forget his tantrums toward us when I was taking part in the usual end of term school concert – my last – in the now demolished Lochend Church. (Incidentally, I only recently discovered that the stained glass windows which once adorned this church are now safely installed in St John's Presbyterian Church in Willis Street, Wellington, New Zealand.) I was in the 'changed voice choir' – all boys, of course – and at our last rehearsal held on the morning of the concert, he was so incensed at our efforts that he literally screamed with temper, and swore that we would not be allowed to sing that night.

We were petrified, certain that he would carry out this threat, but the night came and we who had the last spot in the programme were of course allowed to perform. We sang *Star of the County Down*, *Land of Hope and Glory*, and *Jerusalem*. We sang our hearts out, and the audience would not let us off the stage until we had given two encores of *Jerusalem*. I will never forget Wee

Mickey standing there facing us with tears streaming down his cheeks, at the end. He had dragged us to heights unknown.

A Captain? Without any doubt!

The final major happening which I recall prior to leaving school concerned Neil Campbell, the gentle man who tried against all the odds to teach me and some of my contemporaries, including Cecil Finn, to play the bagpipes.

Neil Campbell also lived in Dalintober. He was a master painter, a tallish man with an inclination to stoop. His oil paintings of Kintyre scenes are well known locally, and are quite collectable. I may well be the only person who ever heard him swear. In his house we tried hard to master the ancient art, whilst he sat puffing at his pipeful of 'thick black', with his fingers over his ears, listening intently at close range to our efforts on the pipes which had been bought – at what financial sacrifice we never knew – by our long-suffering parents.

The bag on Cecil Finn's pipes had rotted beyond redemption, so some of his deceased father's work mates fashioned a new bag – which was more innovative than successful – by vulcanising together the ends of an inner tube from the wheel of a lorry, cut roughly to size and holed to accept the drones, chanter, and mouthpiece. This contrivance had several faults.

One, it was too big for the tartan cover. Two, it was a lurid red colour, and three, it was almost impossible to blow. Indeed, Cecil was the only one who was able to keep the pipes up, and then only for a very limited time.

There came the day when Neilly, as he was affectionately known, entered us in the Junior competition for piping, at Kintyre Park in Campbeltown. We gathered on the day, and our demoralisation was completed by the unkind comments of our contemporaries on seeing us in our kilts, borrowed from who knows where, for the day. Neilly puffed nervously on his beloved pipeful of baccy as he tuned our drones to the best of his ability, and coached us on the ritual of 'placating the judges', which had to be undergone before being allowed to play. The moment arrived.

Cecil marched with apparent boldness to where sat the three ancient judges – seemingly asleep – halted in front of them, and upon seeing a possible move-ment from one of them, saluted smartly. This salute was belatedly acknowledged in a desultory manner by the senior judge, who then demanded to be apprised of Cecil's name. This given – and received with only a derisory snort – Cecil had then to tell them which tune he would play. This information was duly noted by the only judge who gave any indication of being alive, but his scornful reaction gave the impression that such a tune was well beyond the capabilities of this candidate who had dared to approach him, and a casual wave dismissed the competitor who was by now in a state of pure terror. Cecil saluted again, turned, and marched to where he would begin his offering, leaving the judges apparently asleep again. This scene of somnolence was destroyed when one of the judges, perhaps the one currently on watch, suddenly sat bolt upright and abruptly shook the other two into awareness of the sight which was now unfolding before their bleary eyes.

As Cecil blew into the bag, which had hitherto been hidden by being stuffed into the too-small tartan cover, there started to appear from its hiding place a lurid, decidedly phallic, red tube! This appalling sight was obviously beyond the comprehension of the combined experience of the poor men, who were now apparently in the first stages of shock, and who were seemingly unable to give the command to start. Our piper, whose endurance, remember, was somewhat limited, watched them intently. Time, the great healer, did its work; the signal to begin was given, and Cecil started at last. On the wrong foot!

Poor Neilly's pipe almost caught fire, and that was when I heard him swear, but all was not lost – Cecil *was* one of the prize winners.

Neil Campbell is another gentle Captain whose presence around the fireplace of Angus's dreams would indeed be a delight, and whose playing would give much pleasure to many.

Cecil and I could hardly wait to join the bands of those we were desperate to emulate – the young fishermen who flaunted their worldly knowledge before our envious eyes. They had seen places we had only dreamt about: Castlebay, Lochboisdale, Stornoway, Mallaig, Peel, Whitby. Their tales of these far-flung ports were listened to with awe.

I remember while still at school, sitting with two others of like mind in a cafe in Campbeltown one evening, when to our astonishment we were joined by a young fisherman whose attraction for the ladies was the envy of many, especially us pubescent lads whose combined experience of the fair sex totalled absolutely nil, despite our bravado. And he – whom we will call Bill – knew it. He actually deigned to sit down with us, who were usually ignored and deemed to be unworthy of any sort of recognition by such as he, and started to talk.

'What is it like in the North (at the Minch herring fishing)?' we asked him.

'Well,' he replied, 'it can be great fun. We had a good shot of herring in Oban the week before last; aye, the money was good too. That was on the Friday, and we were late finishing so we didn't go out that night. I went to a dance in the Corran Halls where I met a girl, God but she was beautiful.'

He then launched into a detailed physical description of this young lady, which had us drooling in anticipation of things which we felt were yet to come.

'After the dance I walked with her to the farm which was her home, and we went into the barn, a cosy place filled with hay. There was a full moon that night, and the spot where we lay on the hay was fitfully lit by moonbeams coming through a window high on the wall. We kissed passionately.'

A long pause followed, then he slowly described to us how he had caressed her lovingly, and had removed all of her clothes, silken piece by silken piece, until her beautiful body lay in his arms clad only in the soft moonlight. We dwelt on his every word, drooling at the mouth.

'She lay there, her eyes wild and wanting,' he continued, 'then she arched her nubile body against me.'

'Hurt me Bill!' she cried desperately.

By this time he had us totally engrossed, and we were as desperate as she seemed to be for the consummation of this tale. Bill waited.

'What did you do?' called someone in a strangled voice.

9

'What did I do?' concluded Bill as he stood up and drank the last of his tea. 'What do you think I'd do? I gave her a right good slap on the face!'

We never seem to learn.

As young boys we were desperate to experience anything connected with the sea, an obsession which must have caused our parents much worry on occasion. When an old chap named James O'Hara bought several dinghies which had small petrol driven engines to hire out to holidaymakers, we pounced on this opportunity to get our hands on any kind of boat by offering our 'services', as boat minders and general helpers, free of charge. Our persistence bore fruit in that we got a great deal of pleasure when our duties involved moving the dinghies around the harbour for any reason. This gave us a lot of experience of boat handling at a very early age, though our fertile inventiveness in coming up with good reasons for having shifted the dinghies must have stretched his patience to the very limits.

Inner Harbour, Campbeltown

2

The long-awaited day arrived. I left school in December 1950. It was time to start work. Being a fisherman was much more of a pleasure than it is now. Financial and political pressures have placed such demands upon the men pursuing this career, that it is now a very highly stressful, and therefore in my opinion, life-limiting occupation. The political ineptitude of successive leaders has ensured that the future, if indeed there is a future in the fishing industry, is not a rosy one.

Life was quieter then, and men were able to take the time to lavish upon their boats the attention that they deserved. These boats were beautiful in their own right. The curves of their lines were a joy to behold, and the varnished wooden hulls reflected the care taken to keep them looking as they did. The 'ringers', as the boats were called, took their name from the ring-net which they was designed to carry. They were built of wood – usually larch, Oregon or pitch pine planks – on oak frames. The length varied from forty-eight to fifty-eight feet, with a beam the classic one-third-of-the-length, and their draught was in the region of six feet when light. Powered by diesel engines varying in size between the 66 horse- power of the old favourite Kelvin K3 model, and the unbelievable 152 horses of the Gardner 8L3, they were a far cry from the 300-400 horse-power required by similar sized boats to tow the gear they now use.

The configuration was always the same. Accommodation for the crew of six forward, hold amidships, and engine room aft. The wheel house – which by today's standard was small and basic, containing only a steering wheel, a compass, and engine controls – was situated above the engine room, the back of it being about ten feet from the stern. They were designed purely for the pursuit of that king of fish, the herring, and when I started were used almost exclusively for that purpose. The ring-net was so called simply because it was shot in a circle around a shoal of herring.

They carried, dependent on size, from one hundred to over two hundred crans of herring. A cran (four baskets), was a liquid measure which weighed approximately twenty eight stones or 180 kilos, and contained on average around nine hundred fish. The cran was used to quantify the catch on all of the fishing grounds, with the exception of the Clyde. There the measure of the 'basket' – which was simply one quarter of a cran – took over. I do not know why this was; perhaps someone somewhere can tell me! Those ancient standards have both now been superseded by the unimaginatively named 'unit', which is a metric measure of one hundred kilos, foisted upon the industry by the faceless bureaucrats of the ubiquitous EC.

❁

Discharging at Anstruther – mid 1930s
l-r: ??, Sweeney McCrindle, Dick Andrew, Willie Andrew

Almost without exception, the boats were varnished, and every spring when they were scraped to the bare wood, sanded and then re-varnished, there was great rivalry to see what crew by what device could make their boat the best looking one in the fleet! This spring-cleaning was done by the crew of the boat at a time when the fishing was naturally quiet, and although they were sometimes able to claim unemployment benefit, this essential work was undertaken with the knowledge that they would not be paid for it in any way.

As the use of a ring-net required two boats, loose partnerships were formed by skippers of similar personalities. Your partner boat was called your 'neighbour'. The nets which each of these boats carried were in excess of three hundred yards long, and about forty-five yards deep. They were 'shot' around a shoal of herring in a semi-circle. There were corks attached to the backrope of the net for flotation, augmented by five regularly spaced buoys which were around two feet in diameter. When I started fishing, these buoys – referred to as 'bows' – were made of tarred canvas overpainted white for visibility, but were latterly plastic. The bottom of the net, or 'sole rope', was weighted with lead rings.

When shooting the net, one man was positioned aft where he not only saw the net safely over the stern, but called out the progress of the shooting action for the benefit of the skipper who was, of course, fully involved in other matters. "First bow, second bow," (or shoulder) "centre, second last bow" (or second shoulder), "last bow, ease her," – (this if he thought the boat was shooting too fast) – "net's away." This time-honoured chant seldom varied.

The neighbour boat picked up the end of the net which had been dropped by the shooting boat, and after a short (perhaps five minutes) tow to get the net properly into shape, the two boats turned towards one another. The circle was completed when the neighbour boat's crew jumped aboard the shooting boat, taking with them their end of the net, and a towing rope. While the two crews hauled the net, the neighbour boat pulled gently on the tow rope which was attached amidships on the shooting boat, in order to keep her vulnerable propeller and rudder clear of the net.

Not long ago I visited a remote island off the coast of Thailand, and was amazed to discover men on a sandy beach doing repair work on what was without doubt a ring-net. When – with the help of a guide as translator – I questioned them on how they worked it, I was puzzled when it became apparent that there was only one boat involved in its use. Further questioning revealed that they used each shoulder of the boat – instead of pulling the net onto one side of the boat, half forward and half aft as was done here. One half was hauled on to the port side, and the other on to the starboard side. The boat was able to go astern slowly, thus keeping the potentially snagging propeller and rudder well clear of the net. Why didn't we think of that!

It is probably worth recording the duties of the engineer on these boats. He was not required to be technically qualified, but was usually interested in things mechanical. This extra work, which involved running repairs on a day to day basis and keeping the engine and its environs clean, was not financially rewarded in any way. There was a time of course – whilst the mechanisation of the boats was in its infancy – when technical knowledge of engines was difficult to come by. This period was marked by one or two amusing incidents.

On one occasion the engine on one of the boats was not running properly and as the crew were unable to correct the fault, the services of one of the few 'experts' was called upon. He went down into the engine room and, after due deliberation, recognised that the air-to-fuel mixture was not correct, and that therefore the carburettor needed adjustment. The diagnosis made, he told the skipper that the engine was not getting enough air. The relieved skipper rounded on the anxious crew who had all gathered around the hatch leading into the engine room, and roared, 'Hear that boys? Stan' back an' gi'e her air!'

The first engines were called 'go ahead' engines for the simple reason that there was no gearbox, and therefore as soon as the engine was started up the boat drove ahead. Reverse gear was a luxury still to come, and it became a matter of great pride, if not of honour, that this engine be stopped at exactly the correct time when entering a harbour so that the boat coasted gently to her designated berth. To this end, the engineer was positioned in the engine room hatch waiting for the order 'Stop her!'

One skipper, taking his boat into Campbeltown harbour and having given the order to stop the engine, looked at the pier which was crowded with onlookers and suddenly became aware that he had left it too late, that she was carrying far too much way (was going too fast) and would not stop in time to avoid damage. Panic took over from reason.

'Stop her!' he cried in desperation.

'She's stopped!' squealed the equally horrified engineer.

'Well stop her more!' was the last order from the skipper before bedlam was let loose!

The engineer, because of his dirtier job, suffered more than the rest of us from the lack of personal cleaning facilities. My late uncle Crawford, a very meticulous man, was engineer on my father's boat and he devised a method of cleaning oily boiler suits, part of which process involved towing them behind the boat when under way. One day, when entering Lochboisdale after a trip across the Minch, he hauled in the rope to find that his boiler suit was no longer there. He was not amused to hear a wag suggest that a basking shark had taken it! There were no wash basins on the vast majority of the boats, except for the enamel basin in which we washed to the best of our abilities.

On a more delicate subject: although the newer ringers had toilets, on the older boats this most basic of facilities was limited to a metal five-gallon drum. This was made usable by having the top cut off and the resulting ragged edge covered by a piece of hose which was split lengthways and lashed around the drum.

These then were the boats in which we hunted.

I am at a loss to explain to anyone the mystique of the pursuit of herring. That there *is* some sort of mystique is beyond doubt. As evidence of this, although there are literally dozens of poems and songs about the herring, I know of none praising the cod, haddock, whiting or prawn!

The pursuit of herring with a ring-net, meant that the men were much nearer nature than is the case now in the days of computers and sonar sets. An East Coast fisherman told me very recently that he remembered as a young man lying one fine spring afternoon on the pier at Polteil on Skye, in the company of an old fisherman, gazing down into the sea.

'D'ye see anythin' odd aboot this pier,' asked the old chap, 'somethin' that probably means the herrin' fishing'll be late this year?'

My informant admitted that he couldn't see what had come to the notice of the old man. He was told that he should have spotted the absence of barnacles on the wooden legs of the pier, which meant that – to the observant eye – the seasons were running late!

❀

All of the senses, bar one – that of taste – were used in the hunt for herring. Touch was used to feel the herring which were struck by the fine wire that trailed behind the slow moving boat with a heavy lead weight attached. Herring could be heard when they jumped clear of the water – perhaps in an attempt at evading a predator, or when they indulged in the frenzy of 'playing': unexplained behaviour which meant that on a quiet night the rushing sound they made as they splashed on the surface could be heard literally miles away. Sight was used in a great many ways to track the shoals; for example, looking for a gannet 'striking' or diving on a shoal, or merely 'looking well' – a description used when a gannet was seen peering intently downward from a high hovering altitude. We used to chase the poor gannets which were seen sitting heavy in the water, as they would then, in a panic, spew up the contents of their stomachs in order to lighten themselves enough for flight, thus revealing what they had been feeding on.

'Sailfish' or 'muldoans', as we called the basking sharks, fed on the same plankton as herring, so whenever we saw them – and they were relatively common in those days – we cruised among them hoping that there was a shoal of herring there also. Muldoans could cause a lot of damage to the nets if accidentally caught, so a necessary piece of equipment was a can of diesel fuel kept ready for instant use when we thought that they were around. While shooting the net in a semi-circle, the diesel was poured sparingly into the water in the hope that the beasts would dive clear of the foul-tasting stuff, and so clear of the net also. Seeing herring gulls sitting contentedly on the water was a sight interpreted as a sign that herring lay deep below them. We watched intently for a 'change in the water' at night in the summer months, a change brought about by the movement of fish causing a revealing phosphorescent glow. This was usually referred to as 'seeing them in the burning,' or 'seeing them in the water.'

Finally; yes, they could be smelt! A very distinctive raw smell in a loch meant that there was a heavy concentration of fish there. My late uncle Henry Martin was taped by my cousin Angus, relating the following tale.

One lovely summer day they were lying alongside Jim McCreath 'Jimmy the May', whom they were then neighbouring, in Corrodale Bay on the east side of

Uist, discussing what their next move should be.

'There's naethin' here' cried Jimmy. 'Where d'ye think we should go?'

Henry's skipper Willie MacIntyre, better known as 'Screich', called forward to where Henry sat watching a gannet low in against the cliff face.

'Ye're afa' quiet up there Mertin, whoot d'ye think we should dae?'

Henry stated that in his opinion, anyone who left here was going away clear of herring, because he said he could get the 'raa smell o' herrin' in the air.' There was much scoffing about this, Jimmy the May saying, 'Well, if ye can smell herrin', that's a new yin on me. I've heard many's the thing, but I never heard anybody sayin' they could smell them!'

'So we waited,' said Henry, 'an' they started jumpin' in the evenin', an' we shot an' got a good ring, jeest as close tae the rocks as we could get. Jimmy went haywire. "There's a man can smell them!" he says.

'Well, a funny thing. We cam' back there the next day, an' it so happened the fishin' was slack, but there wis a fleet there, boats ringin'. Ye know that smeltins ye get in the watter, an' the smell o' the oily smeltins? Well the place wis polluted. Jimmy cam' alongside, an' he says, "Mertin, there's nae doubt," he says, "the smellin' business is aa right – are ye smellin' that?" Says I "That's gleshins (young saithe) ye're smellin', that's no' herrin'." '

'Now that wis a chancer ye see. I thought the smell wis aafa' strong right enough. Well the *Nobles* an' the *Silver Grey* shot an' got a hunner baskets o' gleshins. That killed him!

'Years later,' he continued, 'I mind o' bein' in the fo'c'sle o' another Ayrshire boat wan day when the talk wis o' herrin' as usual, an' a young lad pipes up "I heard tell o' a Campbeltoon man that could smell herrin' miles away, is that true?" – but I jeest held ma peace an said nothin.'

Henry had a very distinctive deep bass voice, very easy to listen to, and hearing a recording of him reminded me that he had what I would describe as the last Dalintober accent – as opposed to Campbeltown just half a mile away – that I ever heard.

Nothing in his accent came across as *nawthin*, Campbeltown says *naethin*, and *came* was pronounced *cam*, where a Campbeltown accent was more like *kim*. He pronounced aboard as *aboord*. He also used *fornenst* instead of *in front of.* For example – 'Ah was stannin fornenst the winch.' A wonderful old man with a wonderful memory. Why did I not think to tape some of the tales I heard him tell?

Another maternal uncle, Dunky, told me a true story which is well worth repeating, even if it is a wee bit out of place here. I will alter the names but not the content.

He had, Dunky told me, been in school with 'S—', a local worthy who was only sober, in my opinion, when he had no money for drink. As he was not a very savoury character at all, I was surprised to hear that my uncle had always had a soft spot for him. This surprise was lessened when he went on to explain to me that he had been schoolmates with S—, and had always felt that given half a chance, the poor man would not have ended up in the gutter. Dunky continued

16

the tale by telling me that he had never passed this fellow by, but had always given him the time of day, although he was more often drunk than sober and therefore probably didn't recognise Dunky, his old school pal.

One day he met the reprobate, and was told a story which he promptly dismissed as pure fantasy. S— had been on his way back to the hovel he called home, and was by his own admission, drunk. His path took him past a certain establishment from which emanated hymn singing. Dunky quoted him as saying: 'I felt somethin' pullin' me in tae this place, so in ah went, an' stood at the back o' the hall beside a nice young couple. This pair looked at me, an' shifted aweh clear o' me wi' their noses in the air. Ah didna' wait, but jeest went aweh hame.

'The next day,' he continued, 'B— (a prominent local business man) cam' up tae my hoose, wi' his big car, he asks me whit wey ah didna' stay in the meetin', an' he offers tae come for me an' tak' me tae the next meetin' in his car.'

' "No," says I, "whoot ah wis lookin' for wisna' there. Ah'm no' gaan wi' ye." '

Shortly after that, he told Dunky, he had been passing the Salvation Army Citadel in the centre of the town, in his cups again, and had been drawn in by the singing he heard coming out. This time, remembering his reception in the last place, he had gone in very reluctantly and had stood in the passageway at the back of the hall.

'The Captain o' this Army was singin' doon at the front o' the hall, an' dae ye know this Dunky, he cam' up tae me, pit his airm roon me – drunk an' dirty as ah wis – an' took me right doon tae the front wi' him. They gave me tea an' sandwiches, an' took me hame that night in a car. Ah'll nivir touch drink again as lang as ah leeve Dunky, that's it!'

'I had heard him say a thousand times that he was feenished wi' the drink, an' this was only a year or two ago when he wis an old man,' Dunky told me, 'but d'ye know this, fae that day tae the day he died jeest last year, he wis a reformed character. There wis nivir a night went past but wan o' they good folk cam' up tae see him if he wisna' fit tae go tae the meetin, an' he nivir pit a fit wrang!'

One Campbeltown skipper, more noted for the noise he made than for his prowess in catching herring, made his reputation almost immortal by calling to his crew from his place in the wheel house, 'Look and listen with all the eyes and ears God gave you boys, for my home's in a deplorable condition!'

Six years ago I visited Cockenzie, on the Firth of Forth, seeking the Weatherhead boat building yard, the birthplace of so many ringers, but could not identify it. I asked a Mr Murdoch – who, I later discovered, worked in the fish-processing building from which he had just emerged – where I might find it.

The resulting conversation is worth recording, and went thus:

'Weatherhead's yerd, that's it ower there. The last ringer frae there wis the *Watchful*, BA 124, beelt fur a man ca'd Sloan, frae Ayrshire.'

Realising that I had found someone who knew more than I had any right to expect, I asked if he had been at the ring-net fishing?

'No, Ah wisna' but ma faither wis, he hid a share o' a ringer ca'ad the *Budding Rose*. Ah drove ma mither daft when ah wis at the school, ah was jeest desperate tae get oot an' away tae the ringing. The year afore Ah left school ma faither bocht anither boat frae Fife, second han', an' he asked me if ah'd go wi' him tae sail it hame.

' "Aye faither, but we'll be aye ga'an tae the ring-net wi' this boat, will we?"

' "Weel son," he says, "we will, but whiles we'll ha'e tae gang tae the white fish. This is a bigger boat an' we'll need tae pey her quick."

'He widna' budge frae that, so Ah nivir pit ma fit abaird her. Ah widna' gang tae onythin' but the ringing!'

This was not untypical of the feelings of many of the men who were at the job then. There was a feeling – totally unjustified in fact but understandable none the less – that we were hunters, and as such were superior to those who used drift nets to catch the same species we sought, but who – in our biased opinion – simply shot nets and hoped for the best! The men themselves were a quieter more gentle breed, and I am sure that they had much more concern for their fellow-fisherman than seems to be the case now.

That they were not angels, however, is borne out by the oft-repeated tale of the disappearing petrol, a phenomenon which occurred in Campbeltown many years ago.

In the early days of engines, the fuel used was paraffin, but a bottle of relatively expensive petrol was carried for the starting procedure. The bottle full of petrol had been stolen from a particular boat on several occasions. This persistent pilfering had to be stopped, so cunning was put to good use, and one morning the crew whose petrol was disappearing stood at the head of the quay until all the boats except theirs and one other had left for the fishing grounds .

They then wandered quietly down the pier and silently watched the efforts of the remaining boat's crew to start their engine. Eventually one of the men on the quay shouted down to them, 'If ye dae get it started, yer fortune's made. That bottle's full o' watter!'

This then was the occupation into which, all starry-eyed, I entered to become an apprentice to the breed I thought to be a breed apart – the ring-net fishermen.

It was customary at this time that the youngest man on the crew was delegated cook. This was by far the most onerous job on the boat, and I now feel sure that the practice was only accepted by the youngster because the hapless youth was unable to wield enough clout to alter it.

My first trip, on which of course I was cook, was in January 1950 right after I left school at Christmas. We went to the North, which involved going round the Mull of Kintyre, up inside Islay, Jura and Mull, round Ardnamurchan, then north again past the west coast of Skye; through the Sound of Harris we went, to our final destination, West Loch Tarbert in Harris. This loch is completely exposed to the West, and I was horrified at the enormous swell which rolled in on us

Skipper Tommy Ralston, Whitby 1952

MFV *Golden Fleece* CN170 c1950
Forward to aft:
Jock MacKenzie   Peter McShannon   Robert Gillies
Tommy Ralston (wheelhouse)   Crawford Gillies   Charlie Smith

from the North Atlantic. I had been sick all the way, but this did not bring any sympathy from anyone, and I was expected to simply get on with it. Seasickness was just one more cross which had to be borne, and was not accepted as an excuse for not cooking. Anyway, we ate our dinner (such as it was) going through the Sound of Harris, then I had to set to and wash the dishes, although I am quite certain that – after three days of vomiting with an empty stomach – if a doctor had seen me, he would have had me in a hospital. This washing-up chore meant filling an enamel basin (one of a pair of different-coloured enamel basins; the other one was for washing oneself in), which I had put on the table, with hot soapy water. I had just started the dishes, when our neighbour, the *Morag Bhan* shot, so I put the basin and dishes on the floor where they could fall no further, pulled on my oilskin, or 'doaper' as we called it then, and went on deck to help haul the net. Back aboard the *Golden Fleece*, after what had proved to be a vain attempt to catch herring, I took off my oilskin and went below to finish the washing-up. I promptly stood on the basin, and flooded the forecastle floor with what was by now cold, greasy water. I sat down and cried, and if I could have got on to a pier anywhere, that would have been the end of my fishing career!

The cook, in addition to having to take his full share of all the everyday work, was expected not only to cook for six men – having had no formal training – but to keep the living space clean and tidy. This living space, the fo'c's'le, measured about fifteen feet long by around twelve feet wide, and tapered to a point as one went forward toward the stem.

In this tiny area six men lived, ate, and slept for periods of up to six weeks without respite. Their belongings were stored in suitcases kept in the individual bunks, except of course when the bunks were occupied. Then they found space on the platform, as we called the floor of the fo'c's'le. Making breakfast was not made easier by having to clamber around the suitcases while the men remained in bed. The newer boats were much bigger, and some of them actually had what then seemed to me to be the ultimate in luxury: individual lockers for each man to store his personal gear. They also had that most wonderful addition, a gas cooker!

My cooking efforts were accomplished – if that is the correct word – on a coal stove which had a very small oven to one side of the fire, with the additional back-up of a single-burner Primus cooker. This paraffin-powered Primus was set in operation by heating the burner with highly inflammable methylated spirits, and on one occasion the cook was so dazed by lack of sleep that he poured meths on to the hot coal stove. The resulting conflagration quickly woke him up!

Of course, stores also had to be kept in this tiny living area, and when leaving home for the Minches – an adventure we called 'gaan tae the North' – the boat had to be provisioned bearing in mind that no food of any kind would be available in the more remote lochs, for periods of time which no one could predict. Woe betide the poor cook who ran out of any of the basics, no matter what the circumstances.

I spent Christmas Day of 1952 storm-bound at anchor in a tiny loch near Lochmaddy in North Uist. There were three boats tied together, each with chains and anchors out. The wind was howling from the south west, and as was usual with this kind of gale, the rain was driving past us in horizontal torrents. I remember sitting alone in the wheel house with the radio tuned to a BBC outside broadcast from a children's hospital somewhere, listening to the sounds of merriment and wondering, as I looked at the scene of desolation all around, just why I hadn't listened to my mother's pleas to get a job ashore! Anyway, at about eleven o'clock in the morning, we slipped our chain aboard one of the other boats and went to the pier at Lochmaddy. There was too much motion to lie alongside the exposed pier without doing damage to the boat, so with my uncle Crawford at the wheel, we put our stem to the pier, and my father jumped ashore. He came back soon bearing three bottles of whisky; we approached, he jumped aboard, and we were off back to anchor again, where he passed a bottle to each of the other boats.

Christmas dinner on that day was a steak pie, made with tinned steak and covered with pastry made by my father, who was quite a good baker. He thought up some pretext to get the rest of the crew on deck, swore me to secrecy and used his shaving brush to paint tinned milk on to his pastry to glaze it! Tinned soup, potatoes and tinned peas, followed by tinned rice and tinned fruit completed the feast, and was pronounced 'great' by the unsuspecting crew, but before we ate he produced our bottle of whisky and emptied it into six glasses. He then looked long at me, pronounced: 'One in the family is enough to be drinking' – and scoffed mine along with his own!

Yes, being cook on my father's boat, the *Golden Fleece*, carried no privileges!

Likewise, if there was a defect found in the engine room I was usually blamed, even though I was the cook, and might well have been busy at the stove at the time the fault manifested itself!

The storage of drinking water was another problem. The tank, which was quite small, had to be filled at every opportunity, usually by carrying the water from a tap on the pier, or from a convenient well if there was no tap, to the boat, in a flask which held about five gallons. This again was the responsibility of the cook, and the task of carrying this heavy metal container was expected to be shared with the cook of your 'neighbour' boat. Presumably this job was considered to be beneath the dignity of the other crew members, or perhaps they had done enough of this kind of work when they were cooks themselves!

The 'boy', as the cook was invariably called, was also charged with the job of knowing where his neighbour was at any time during the searching part of the fishing operation, and had to watch this boat very carefully. This was a very important task because when the neighbour boat was about to shoot her net, the end of it – which was marked with a very small lit buoy called a 'winkie'– had to be picked up immediately. Your skipper therefore had to be informed at once. The only indication of this imminent activity was the sudden appearance of a light on the fore end of his wheel house, which was not easily seen. This tiny light was called a winch-light. The flashing of any bright lights was thought to frighten the herring so, if the dim winch-light was not spotted at once, and the shooting boat had to draw attention to her activities by using a searchlight flashed at her neighbour, then the poor offending boy was in trouble once more! This watch was relatively easy to keep in the lonely lochs of the North, but became very difficult in the crowded waters of the Manx or Whitby fisheries where many boats worked in congested areas. This congestion led to the addition of very many – totally illegal – lights, designed solely to make the task of recognition easier. I often wonder just what went through the minds of the skippers of coasters when they were confronted with the myriad of double stern lights and the vast variety of multi-coloured masthead lights of a fleet of ringers?

In the Isle of Man and the Whitby fisheries, where we worked among boats from the East Coast, life was further complicated by the fact that East Coast ringers worked their nets from the starboard side, whilst we used the port side. This meant that if a boat was seen by its lights to have its net in the water, one never knew which side of that boat to pass, in order to keep clear of the net which he had shot.

The boy was only relieved from his watching task when he had to make a cup of tea. This tea was normally all that was required by the men during the short hours of darkness at the Isle of Man or Whitby fishings. On more than one occasion I used the pretext of making a cup – always acceptable to the crew – when I had lost our neighbour. I would say to one of them 'Watch our neighbour, that's him there. I'm going to make a cup of tea.' A vague pointing gesture in the general direction of the most crowded bunch of lights visible, and then I would scuttle below before he could ask any questions!

Another task, though not solely that of the cook, was to question other boats' success or lack of it if they passed closely enough to be hailed; this was, of course, before the advent of VHF radio. This querying is interesting when one looks back, because it all happened in a language used by Clyde fishermen, the nuances of which would not be understood nowadays. The interrogatory call, 'Puckle the night?', would be answered according to the luck – or lack of it – of the crew questioned, and the replies ran thus:

'No no,' meant nothing at all. A 'wheen o' baskets' was less than a 'puckle o' baskets', which in turn – strange to relate – was somewhat less than 'a wee wheen'! The reply 'a wee puckle' was shouted in a rather smug tone, signifying that Lady Luck had smiled upon the questioned boat. Finally, 'a good puckle' meant that the informant would soon be off on his way to market, as this was a well-fished boat. There were also of course the definitive replies – for example, 'a hunner baskets!'

Questioning the crew of a successful boat as to just what method had been used to find the herring which they had caught, provided another example of a form of language which no longer exists.

The query, 'How did ye feel them?', would, on occasion, be answered by what to the uninitiated would appear to be the sarcastic reply 'We saw them in the watter!' This simply meant that they had seen the herring in the 'burning'.

On one occasion, when a large fleet were meeting with very little success, the

22

bored crew of a boat, when questioned by the skipper as to what the replies were, changed them so that it appeared to the poor man that he was the only one who had caught no herring. Their arrival in Tarbert the following morning brought the realisation that this lack of success was by no means unique, and provoked another famous row, when their skipper realised that the crew had been winding him up!

Payment of the crews was, and still is, strictly by results. No fish meant no money! When fishing away from home, crews were often given 'subs' at the weekend – a cash advance geared to the skipper's estimate of the amount grossed that week. From this, each man was expected to send money home to his wife, and of course to buy cigarettes etcetera for the coming week. When fishing at home, the skipper 'divided' the net earnings every Saturday. There were eight and a half shares in this computation in a boat which carried a crew of five men and a boy – one for each crew man, half for the boy, and one each for the boat, engine, and nets. Crew wives spoke to one another about the earnings – or lack of them – so there were not many opportunities for the men to 'skin off' a few pounds for a dram or two. One enterprising chap, who had married a girl from outwith the fishing community, hit upon the idea of deducting a pound or two every few weeks, telling his unsuspecting spouse that it had been his turn to buy the baskets which were used to discharge the catches. These baskets were in reality, of course, paid for out of the gross earnings. This scheme worked well until the man got a bit too greedy, and his wife complained to the skipper's wife about the obviously deteriorating quality of the baskets, which now seemed to have to be replaced weekly!

Practical jokes were commonplace then as now, and I well remember hearing of the cruel trick played upon an old chap whose eyesight was so bad that he had shipped as cook on one boat, feeling that he was no longer fit to be a deckhand. He had laid a 'fry' of plaice on the wooden floor of the hold, clear of the attentions of the hungry seagulls, until it was time to cook them. One of the crew, seeing this, nailed the flat fish to the floor, reducing the poor old chap to the verge of tears when he tried to lift them!

Another trick, which did not immediately end in laughter, was played not too long ago in Eyemouth.

Two brothers who owned seine-netters and who fished very well, decided to treat their hard-worked crews and their wives to dinner when they stopped fishing for Christmas. This dinner became an annual occasion which was relished by all concerned. One day one of the crew had started celebrating early in the afternoon, and went home somewhat the worse for wear to find his wife getting dressed for the big event. She was not at all amused by his lapse, and told him so in no uncertain terms. Dressed, they set off for the hotel hosting the dinner, where they were ushered into the cocktail bar to meet the rest of the guests. The poor man sat down, and promptly fell asleep. When they were called to go to the dining room, his wife – still incensed – would not allow anyone to waken him, so he was left sound asleep. One of his crewmates, however, went back to the bar on some pretext or other, unzipped the fly on the poor chap's trousers, and therein placed the neck of a turkey which he had purloined from the hotel kitchen, in such a position that it protruded from the fly. The wife, having finished her soup, suffered a fit of remorse, and went to waken her spouse, entering the bar just in time to see the hotel cat – which had climbed on to the lap of her sleeping husband – start to eat the turkey neck. The poor woman screamed and fainted, cutting her head on one of the tables as she fell! Those men worked hard, and played just as hard!

I well remember, when I was about sixteen, having three Lancashire miners who were on holiday on the Isle of Man, come out with us for the night to see what the job was like. One of them, who was quite small in stature but built very broadly, was extremely sick all night. I did my best to look after him, mainly because it was a novelty to see someone else suffer as I so often had. They went ashore at Peel in the morning feeling very sorry for themselves, and returned in the early evening before we sailed, the small one bearing a gift of sweets for me by way of thanks. He gripped me by the hand, and said in the most heartfelt tone, 'There just isn't enough money in the world to pay you guys – I just couldn't do your job, no matter what the pay.' This came from a man who, with his fellow miners, had described to us how one of the seams they mined was so lacking in height that they actually had to lie on their sides on the wet stone whilst wielding their picks! Not enough money in the world?

There was another occasion which springs to mind about taking visitors to sea with us, but this time the location was Whitby. A local lady who ran a fish and chip shop was in the market for the odd cod which was caught among the herring, and as this was a welcome source of pocket money for the young lads, she was well known to us all. One day she asked me if her daughter could come out with us some night. She was, the lady explained, an actress, and was appearing briefly in the local theatre, the Whitby Spa. Hearing that the subject of the request was an actress – with all the stories we had heard of actresses – guaranteed the trip.

The appointed evening came around, and the fish and chip lady appeared with a stunning beauty, whose appearance confirmed all of our wildest hopes. Safely aboard, she won the hearts of all, as she drifted around wafting the most exotic perfume we had ever smelled. We danced attendance upon her every whim, and when she eventually declared that she was a little weary and desired to rest for a while, one of my older and infinitely more worldly-wise shipmates beat me to the punch, and offered his bed for her to rest in.

I hated him.

When we arrived back in Whitby, and the beauty had gone home to her mother taking our hearts with her, we prepared for bed ourselves. Great was the delight of this shipmate (who will not be named), as he related to us in great detail the dreams which were in store for him when he laid his head on the pillow which, as he demonstrated, was redolent of her perfume. Even greater were his roars when he eventually clambered into his bed to discover that it was

24

soaking wet. He never lived it down!

Because of a self-imposed ban on Sunday fishing, work for the week was finished as soon as the Friday night catch had been discharged on the Saturday morning, and the rest of the weekend was free for leisure pursuits. The Isle of Man was a favourite with all the young unmarried men, and it was quite common for one of the pair of boats to set off home on the Saturday morning with all of the married men from the pair on board, leaving the other boat to go into Peel with the young single lads.

Dancing was the 'in' thing then, and if one was to have any success with the fair sex, it was essential to be reasonably accomplished in the art of ballroom dancing. We all fancied ourselves as budding Fred Astaires, and it came as something of a shock when my wife and I met an old flame of mine from those days, only for her to say to my wife, 'He thought he was a good dancer then, but we hadn't the heart to tell him otherwise!'

This need to be a reasonably proficient dancer meant that it was foolish to take too much to drink. All we usually had was enough to give us courage to make that dreaded long, lonely journey across the dance floor from the 'man's side' of the hall, to the other side where – dressed in their party best – stood the aloof girls pretending they didn't see us coming! Anyone the worse for wear stood little chance of being accepted as a dance partner, so would not be able to pose the vital question, 'Can I see you home tonight?' to the girl of his choice. Another long, lonely walk back to the boat was all that was left to the unfortunate fool who drank too much.

The year's toil began in May when all the boats – looking beautiful after two months of varnishing and painting – set off for the North. This fishing, one of the few conducted in daylight when the herring were up feeding on surface plankton, lasted until the early part of June, when the Manx season began. In late August we set off through the now sadly defunct Forth and Clyde Canal, to Seahouses and Whitby. Not much time was spent fishing around Campbeltown, which meant that none of us experienced a home life worthy of the name. We got home from the North around one weekend per month, but weekly from the Isle of Man, if we had herring on the Saturday which merited a trip to Portpatrick, thus taking us halfway home. It was rare indeed for anyone to get home from the six weeks or so spent in Whitby.

The Forth and Clyde Canal ran from near Grangemouth on the Forth, to Bowling on the Clyde, and en route skirted Falkirk and Glasgow, exciting country for young lads. I remember looking for the landmark of the clock – which was then reputed to be the biggest in the world – above the Singer factory in Glasgow. As I write, I hear that the 'Powers that Be' are being pressed to re-open the canal at great cost. It should not have been closed in the first place, in my opinion. The Yorkshire fishing lasted until late September, and the return to Campbeltown meant a quick touch up to the varnish and a bottom clean before setting off again for the North where we remained until the end of February or the beginning of March. There was then a short spell of fishing around the south end of Arran, or on the Ballantrae Banks off the Ayrshire coast, before it was time for the boats to be beached in Campbeltown to scrape and varnish before a new year began.

This lack of time in Campbeltown did not bother me, a young single man; but it must have been a strain on a marriage where for a great part of the year the wife had to be a father to the family in addition to her normal motherly tasks.

Map of Scotland and N England showing places mentioned in this book

3

Jock MacKenzie, or 'Kenzie' as he was known, was just about the most expert and dedicated fisherman I ever worked with. He was a round sturdy man, not very tall, with very fixed habits and ideas. An individual who, for example, would not eat a fried egg which had not been salted in the pan whilst cooking, and for whom herring – a staple food – had to be boiled for *exactly* twenty minutes!

He never left the deck at any time when fishing was taking place. Prior to leaving the harbour, Jock would fill all of his pipes with baccy, make sure that they were all drawing to his satisfaction, and then stow them carefully – bowl up – at the side of his bunk. When he felt the need for nicotine, there came the dreaded call 'Light my pipe boy.' He would not strike a match himself, thus preserving his night vision, but many times in my imagination I destroyed much more than his vision, such was my loathing for these foul-tasting abominations !

During the summer nights he lay on the starboard side of the bow, an old mallet in his hand, with which he would strike the top rail from time to time. This blow sent a shock wave through the water, startling any herring which were too deep to be disturbed by the boat passing. The resultant movement of the fish stirred the phosphorescence in the water, causing a faint glow deep down which revealed their presence. This task demanded total concentration and a very keen eye, as well as great experience. 'Ease her down!' he would call to my father in the wheelhouse, then in an aside to me – 'Did you see that, boy?' 'Aye Jock,' I would reply – but on many occasions seeing the dim glow deep down took far more experience than I had gained. It would also be fair to say that my eyes were closed in fitful sleep more often than not as I lay on the foredeck, because the fleshpots and bright lights of Whitby and the Isle of Man were a sore temptation to a young lad who should have been sound asleep in his bunk!

He was the only man I ever knew who called for the net to be shot in the month of January, in the Minch, saying that he had seen a 'wee scatter in the burnin'.' Those of us who knew that no one could see any herring in the winter months in the burnin' (as we called the phosphorescence), were put firmly in our places when the first herring was spotted meshed in the wide wings of the net shot as a result of his observation!

At the Whitby fishing the fleet used to leave harbour in the early evenings en masse on their way to the grounds between Whitby and Scarborough, and the quay would be thronged with holidaymakers viewing what must have been a wonderful sight.

One evening my father had fallen by the wayside, and was still in the pub long after the last boat had left, leaving only us and our neighbour, the *Glen*

Carradale, still tied to the pier.

The skipper of the *Glen Carradale*, 'Wee Alec' McBride, would much rather have been fishing around the Pluck (a point of land close to his home in Carradale) and the absence of my father was all the ammunition he required to re-state his objections to being so far away from home.

He rolled up and down the deck of his boat, his burly figure swaying from side to side exaggerating his anguish, calling to all from whom he thought he would get sympathy.

'He's a hellova man that Tommy Tit. Up there boozin' and us lyin' here wi' the rest o' the fleet at the sea. We'd be far better off at hame than lyin' here lik this. Oh my God, is this no' jeest terrible!'

On and on it went, with myself feeling most unhappy at his seeming miscalling of my father, yet too young and inexperienced to do anything about it, until at last my father rolled down the quay and we were able to go to sea .

It was dark now of course, but as soon as we had cleared the harbour Kenzie was up at his usual station, although everyone knew that no one caught any herring until they had reached the grounds which were at least eight miles from Whitby. Everyone except Kenzie. The herring were there that night, and all the fleet had passed over them in daylight!

'Stand by,' roared Kenzie from his post at the bow.

We shot, and two hours later were back in the still-deserted harbour, with the night's quota safely stowed below.

'Aye, ye're a hellova man althegether Tommy,' was now the cheerful call from Wee Alec as he strutted up and down the deck grinning from ear to ear, all thoughts of the Pluck gone. 'Ye've the luck o' the Devil right enough!'

I did not give Kenzie proper recognition for his professionalism till many years later. A Captain indeed.

One of the most disagreeable facts of life at the fishing in the summer time was having to put up with scowders, the stinging jellyfish which were the source of much pain to all. When hauling, the nets became liberally coated with their highly irritating tendrils. These became airborne when the net was shaken to get rid of the herring which were meshed in it. The stinging which resulted from these airborne particles hitting exposed skin was very painful. There was no real way to get rid of it, although some swore by washing the afflicted parts with methylated spirit. I have seen men wear plastic face masks when hauling, in a vain attempt at escaping the stings, and it was not unknown for a piece of twine to be attached to the relevant place on one's anatomy, to avoid being stung there when answering a call of nature!

Different nets were used for the winter and the summer fisheries. When one fishery was finished, the net (in those days made of cotton) which had been in use was steeped in a preservative called bark or cutch, which was derived initially from the bark of *Acacia* trees and latterly from a distillation of the wood of the same tree, and which was melted in hot water to make a brew which looked like very strong tea. They were afterwards dried thoroughly by hanging them from poles specially erected for the job, and then stored until next required. So persistent was the sting of the scowder that, when taking the net from the store after perhaps eight months, the dust from the nets stung just as badly, and gave us a reminder of what we were now about to face again !

Whilst on 'medical' matters, I recall hearing of a wonderful truth uttered by a famous – or rather infamous – local worthy who revelled in the nickname of Doosan. He looked in one night on the local consulting room, where sat the sick in mind and body, waiting to be consoled by one of the doctors on duty. Now, if you look around the waiting room of a similar establishment, paying particular attention to the demeanour of the other occupants, you will see very few smiling faces. Doosan looked around the twenty or so patients carefully, then roared, 'What a miserable lookin' shower o' buggers. There's no' wan o' ye but what a good shite wad dae ye the world o' good!'

In the days when I was cooking, a great source of information was from one's watchmate. There were few boats equipped with radio transmitters or receivers in the first year or so of my apprenticeship, so the hours spent on watch during a passage were made less wearying by yarning, or rather in listening to the yarns of the older men. In fact the best watchmates were invariably the best yarners!

One such was 'Lofty' McIntyre, who I always remember with pleasure. Quite a tall man, of spare build, he always seemed to have a wry grin on his face, and was in his element dispelling gloom with a cheery word. I dearly wish that I had kept a diary in those days for I have forgotten most of what I was told, but I remember Lofty telling me some of the adventures which befell him during the war.

He was, he told me, a Seaman/Gunner aboard a mine-sweeping trawler, and one day was on duty as Quartermaster and was steering the mine sweeper when she was strafed by an enemy aircraft. This aircraft was spotted approaching from the starboard side with its forward gunner firing as the aircraft approached.

'Man the port Oerlikon, Lofty!' was the shouted order from the Officer on watch.

Lofty obeyed this order, understanding that the idea was for him to open fire on the aircraft as it climbed away from its attack, using one of the guns mounted on each wing of the bridge. However, he looked back into the wheel house just in time to see the Officer, who had grabbed the steering wheel from him, drop to the deck behind the dubious shelter of the binnacle.

As Lofty surveyed his own totally exposed position and decided he didn't like what he saw, he immediately jumped down on to the engine room casing, where he got equally dubious shelter behind the funnel, from the incoming hail of bullets. As the aircraft pulled up and away on the ship's port side, the rear gunner opened fire on the trawler, using tracer bullets.

The Officer obviously risked a quick glance, and on seeing the tracer, made the mistake in the heat of the moment of thinking that Lofty was firing. Ducking

Robert Robertson of Campbeltown: pioneer ringnet skipper

Tarbert, Loch Fyne. *c*1900:
Duncan Blair (r) – putting a ringnet into a small boat, probably to take
it across to the netpoles, seen in the background, for drying

back behind the binnacle he roared, 'Bloody good show, Lofty. I can see them going right up his arse!'

One foggy night as we were approaching the Mull of Galloway en route to Portpatrick with a shot of herring, Lofty said 'This is no' right fog. I mind wance when I was on the Murmansk run, bein' sent up the foremast tae the crow's-nest tae keep a lookout for German battleships. Well I was up there so long that when I cam' doon, the boat was gone!' He also told me that the seas were so big up there in the Arctic, that they were three days running off the back of one wave!

The risk of being killed or drowned in action was far higher on the mine-sweeping trawlers which had been commandeered from the fishing fleets, than on ships which had been specifically designed for warfare, so in order to preserve some of the lives at risk, the wearing of lifejackets was rigorously enforced. Lofty told me that for years he had worked, eaten, and slept with this one lifejacket around his neck. Burdened with it, like the Ancient Mariner with the Albatross, and loathing its presence just as much, he was allowed to take it off only when leaving the ship to go on shore leave.

He was, he said, on watch-keeping duty whilst the ship was at anchor in Portsmouth harbour, when the official word came through that the war in Europe was over. The lights came on ashore, there were the sounds of celebration from all around, and Lofty, having celebrated modestly – he was on watch remember – returned to his lonely post on deck.

There he leant on the rail seeing the lights, so long darkened, now reflected in the black waters below. Nostalgia took the place of euphoria, and his memory went back over the long weary years of war, the good friends he had made and lost, all the waste of killing he had witnessed; and then casting around in his mind for some positive way of marking what should be a joyous occasion, he remembered the hated lifejacket. He removed it. Looked at it long. Permitted himself a few more moments of pure delight, and threw it in a last gesture of defiance, down into the sea below.

It sank!

Lofty might not make it to Captain, but his company and his yarns would grace those around the fire in Angus's dreams, and if I were there, I'd listen more carefully this time.

Another favourite watchmate from my very young days as a fisherman was Dennis McKay, better known as 'Old Dubs' for some obscure reason. A lovely singer, the usually long watches seemed to flash past when listening to his old songs, or stories from his younger days.

One day we were going round Kilmory Point, which is at the northmost tip of Rum, and which was better known to the Clyde fishermen as 'Dirty Point' because a reef of rocks runs not, as one would expect, straight off the point, but at an angle to it. Dubs told me that, long ago, a couple had lived in the ruined cottage which is still visible on the green sward above the beautiful beach which lies inside the reef. They had seven children. Those children were taken from them one at a time by the then deadly diphtheria, and after burying them just behind the cottage, the distraught couple had left the island, never to return. The story seemed to me to be confirmed when, looking at an old Admiralty chart of the area I saw, marked just where Dubs had indicated, the legend '*graves*'.

Many times after that, when rounding Kilmory, my mind turned to what I had been told, and I imagined the utter despair which must have been felt by the poor parents as they helplessly watched their children die. No telephone, no doctor, no helicopter, no lifeboat – just death in a lonely place. What, I wondered, were their thoughts as they left, and where did they go? At the back of my mind remained the hope that the story was fiction, and that the graves were not of the children.

About fifteen years ago there appeared in the *Scots Magazine*, an article on Rum. In it the writer described visiting Kilmory and related the story just as I had heard it. Reading this brought back all the despair I had felt, but worse still removed all the forlorn hopes I had entertained that it was not true.

A couple of issues later my delight knew no bounds when they printed a letter from a lady in New Zealand, who said that although she had greatly enjoyed the article about Rum, she wished to correct the writer on one detail. The children at Kilmory had *not* all died. Four of them had survived the ordeal of illness, and subsequent migration to New Zealand. There the parents had another three children, bringing the total back to seven.

This she knew for certain, because her grandfather was one of the family which had been born on Rum! I'd dearly love to be able to tell Old Dubs the happy ending to his tale, if I were privileged to meet him at Angus's fireside.

I soon arrived at the age when National Service reared its head. As fishermen, we were not obliged to do the statutory two years in one of the Services, which was the lot of others less fortunate. We could opt to join the Royal Naval Reserve instead. This meant undergoing an initial training period of twenty-eight days, followed by fourteen days every year, for ten years. Of course, we all jumped at the idea of annual 'paid holidays', and I must say that I did enjoy my time there.

My initial training took place in the Naval Barracks at Chatham, and I went in company with Jackie McGeachy from Campbeltown (whose father Sweeney owned the *Margaret Newton*) and 'Baldy' Black from Tarbert, a tremendous character who, sadly, died very young indeed.

We arrived at what, I later discovered, was a bad time: mid-afternoon on a Sunday – time when regular sailors were sleeping off the effects of their tot of rum. The Petty Officer who dealt with our entry into Service life was not amused at having his siesta spoiled, and found great difficulty in coping with Jackie's surname, a difficulty which was shared by almost all of his fellow Englishmen! When, in reply to his query as to where we had come from, we answered 'Campbeltown', he threw his pen on to the floor and bellowed, 'I don't want any of your bloody tricks here. I've had enough of you people.' The reputation of some of our predecessors had obviously made a big impression on him!

Baldy was a little older than Jackie and I, and, being vastly more experienced in the ways of the world, was more able to cope with the pressures of life there. This became obvious when we went on our first parade – on the hallowed parade ground!

It had obviously been discovered that fishermen could not readily cope with marching, so we were ushered quietly into our designated area long before the other Naval personnel – told to stand to attention and neither to move nor speak. In due course, the rest of the parade were marched smartly into place to the strains of the Royal Marine Band, and the Captain appeared, followed by his retinue of attendants. To the justifiable horror of the Petty Officer in charge of our squad of Reservists – of which there were around twenty in number – the Captain made a beeline for us!

I for one became more petrified with each step which brought him nearer, amazed by the array of brilliant gold braid, and dazzled by the glittering drawn swords of his escort. He paused in front of . . . yes, Baldy, and in a very cultured accent inquired as to where Baldy hailed from. On being told, 'Tarbert, Sir', he then said, 'Oh, Tarbert Loch Fyne. What a beautiful place. I sail my yacht there often.' Then, no doubt wondering just what kind of fishing our hero pursued he asked, 'And what were you before you came here?'

Baldy instantly replied with a guileless grin, 'I wis happy, Sir!'

Years later I attended the Petty Officer's training School, HMS *Royal Arthur*, which was oddly situated many miles from the sea in Corsham, a lovely little Wiltshire village. There I came across one of the great characters who were, at that time, the backbone of the Navy. On Church Parade, or Divisions as they were known, denominations other than the Church of England were normally invited to leave the parade ground before the service started by the time-honoured call, 'Fall out RCs (Roman Catholics) and other denominations.' This character, a Chief Gunnery instructor, would bellow from his position on the dais which we faced, 'Fall out RCs, Parsees, Hottentots and Church of Jocks.' I suppose that some do-gooder would object to this now as being an invasion of human rights, or some other such nonsense.

One branch of the Navy which made an enormous impression on me was the gunnery branch, particularly the instructors. Their bearing and turnout was immaculate in every respect, and a visit to the hallowed ground which bred these martinets, Whale Island, was a revelation.

No-one walked anywhere within this establishment at any time; they doubled! Their parade ground was sacrosanct, and the only time anyone put a foot on to it was while on parade.

One day, when running from one class to another, and thinking I was not being observed, I cut across a corner of this ground. There was an unearthly eldritch screech from a Chief Gunnery Instructor across the square:

'Come here. *You*, sailor!'

In terror I ran around, and halted in front of him.

'Who told you to halt? Double mark time! Who gave you permission to cross my parade ground? Don't speak to me you horrible person.'(This when I tried to explain.)

This tirade was delivered from beneath the brim of a Guards-style cap, with the wearer's nose about six inches from mine – in a high pitched scream which could have been heard miles away – and which served only to complete my total demoralisation.

'That is *my* parade ground and I only allow *one* person on it apart from me,' the screams continued. 'The other person is God, and I only tolerate *Him* because I can't see Him!'

No doubt Baldy would have been able to think of an answer, but I was alone and greatly afraid.

I think it was Baldy who told me of one of the MacDougall brothers, famed ring-net exponents from Tarbert Loch Fyne, who was called to serve in the Royal Navy during the war. He was sent to train in the Patrol Service, the branch of the Navy formed to man the fishing boats which had been requisitioned into the Fleet.

On hearing that MacDougall had been in charge of the engine on his boat at home, it was ordained that he, in company with a few others, should take an exam which, if completed successfully, would mean his advancement to Petty Officer Engineman.

He duly took his place in the examination room, the question papers were handed out, and the examinees were told to begin work. The invigilator, a Lieutenant Engineer, curious at the seeming lack of activity from our candidate, approached, looked over the man's shoulder, and saw a sheet of pristine paper. On enquiring into the reason for this inactivity, he was treated to the loud statement 'Ah've been drivin' engines for fifteen years Jeck, an Ah nivir needed a bit o' paper tae start wan o' them yet!'

4

There are I think, remarkable similarities to be seen when considering the Ayrshire and Kintyre fishing communities.

There are three villages, or towns, on each side of the Clyde. The northernmost ones, Tarbert in Kintyre and Dunure in Ayrshire, are similar in size, and their inhabitants are more garrulous and aggressive than their immediate neighbours to the south. Carradale and Maidens are the central villages on the western and eastern shores of the Clyde, and their residents tend generally to be quieter, gentler, and more softly spoken than their neighbours on either side. The two remaining towns, Campbeltown and Girvan, are by far the largest on their respective coasts. They are the southernmost fishing settlements, and their populations shared the dubious distinction of having a much harsher sounding accent than their immediate northern neighbours. They also, in my opinion, tended generally to be much more noisy and quarrelsome than any of the others.

Tarbert Loch Fyne must be the first port of call in the rounds of fishing strongholds, mainly because it is there that the ring-net was first developed in the pursuit of herring in Scotland. A small village on the narrow neck of land which marks the northern boundary of 'God's Country' – Kintyre – it has been blessed with what must be one of the best natural harbours in the world. It has also given birth to more than its fair share of what can only be called 'fishers extraordinary'.

The MacDougalls of Tarbert – Donald, Archie and Peter – referred to in the last chapter, who owned the *Mairerad*, and the *Fionnaghal*, must be immediate candidates for Captaincy. They were commonly known as the 'Ghosts', a collective nickname derived from their habit of using paper to obscure their navigation lights, which was done for several purposes.

Firstly, that the brightness should not scare the herring off the shore where it was hoped that they could be trapped; secondly, that it would lessen the chance of destroying the night vision of the skipper, who wanted to get as close to the shore as possible; and finally, it had the bonus of not betraying their presence to their rival fishermen! It was said of them, 'Ye'd need a light tae see their lights!'

The favourite hunting ground of the Ghosts, when fishing in the North, was Shepherds Bight, a small bay on the east coast of South Uist about two miles south of Loch Skiport. On more occasions than I care to think of, the fleet would race out of the usual anchorage in Loch Skiport as darkness approached in the winter evenings of the 1950s, and try to beat one another into all the favourite herring haunts – south along the shore of the Uists towards Loch Boisdale. The Ghosts took part in the beginnings of these races, but always seemed to drop out early.

In fact they turned their backs on the mad scramble to the south just as soon as they could, wandered unseen back north, and when they could crawl dead slow on their own terms into their preferred Shepherds Bight, they did so. In the early mornings when the reports of the efforts of others began to filter through, very often we heard that, 'The Ghosts are away full up fae somewhere north.'

They were also noted for their habit of making their own anti-fouling paint with which they would cover the bottoms of their boats. The recipe for this was kept secret, but was generally thought to consist of any unused paint, gloss or flat, mixed up in an old barrel. To this was added sheep dip, the ingredient which killed off the unwanted 'galbhin crechachs' (I think that is how it is spelt), or barnacles to anyone not of Tarbert extraction.

If only they could be invited to tell their secrets at Angus's fireside!

It would not be possible to leave Tarbert without mention of that other family of fishers supreme, the Jacksons, who owned the *Oak Lea*, the *Village Maid* and the *Village Belle*. In the days when telephones were a rarity indeed, one of the great sources of news was the milkman. On his rounds with his horse and cart, he got to know all of the gossip in a village, and it was from him that wives got much of the news of the success – or lack of it – of their husbands at the fishing. Tarbert men used to laughingly say, 'Aye, ye'll be namely at the milk cart in the mornin,' whenever anyone did something of note. Well, the Jacksons were namely on a fair few mornings. It was said of them that 'they'd get a shot (of herring) on a patch of damp grass.' I stood in such awe of these men, that I almost believed it!

Another great character from Tarbert, was Willie 'Gorrie' MacAffer. I remember listening one day to a company of what were to me 'old men' yarning aboard the *Golden Gleam* in Castlebay, the subject being the bad weather they had severally experienced in their lives at sea.

As the yarns went around, the seas grew greater and the winds wilder. To quote one unforgettable description, 'There was a bound'(Kintyre expression for a swell), 'aye, a bound up tae the heather.' Willie listened to these tales, his pipe drawing well, smiling very gently as the seas and the stories grew taller.

At last a lull developed in the conversation. Willie, sensing with the unerring instinct of a master that the time was right for the kill, drew deeply on his pipe, fixed his eye on the heavens and said slowly, 'Ah mind wan night gaan across the mooth o' Snizort. Aye, the win' was screamin. Southeast it wis.

'Ah had ma heid oot o' the wheelhoose winda there lookin', lookin' for the land. Well,' (a long pause to ensure that the pipe was drawing properly), 'well, she took wan roll tae starboard, dipped ma pipe intae the watter, an' pit it oot!'

As I remember it, the company dispersed quietly then. I had spent some time with a superb storyteller, and a Captain to boot.

Aboard the *Watchful* at Ayr

(l-r): Andy Alexander, Billy McCrindle, Matt Sloan, Deirdre Sloan, Hugh Alexander, Jimmy Gibson, John Watson

Coming south along the Kintyre shore on our quest for the Captains, about whose exploits I never tired of hearing, but unfortunately forgot far too much, we come to Carradale. This small and beautiful little village is about half way between Tarbert and Campbeltown, but until relatively recently, when a new pier was built, it did not afford a safe harbour for any of the boats owned and operated from it.

I am instantly reminded of 'Wee Jamie' Campbell, owner of the *Irma*, who was probably more in tune with nature than any other fisherman I ever met.

I can still see him, standing outside his cottage beside the burn at Waterfoot near Carradale; a medium-sized, stocky man, dressed – as were all the fishermen from this era – in the home-knitted blue 'gansey'. (These jerseys, by the way, were all knitted by the wives to their own unique pattern. This individuality was deliberate, in the knowledge that it might be the only method of identifying the wearer if he were to be drowned, and the body recovered after some time in the sea.) Wee Jamie rarely had to leave home for the other fisheries exploited by so many of his contemporaries. He did well enough on his home grounds, and at the end of the year when the league table of financial results were being discussed, he was rarely out of the top ten.

Echo sounding devices were in their infancy at this time, and fishermen still relied very much upon the traditional methods of fish-finding, including the feeling wire. This was about thirty fathoms of piano wire, to which was attached a heavy lead weight. The device was trailed astern of the slow moving boat, reached down to about fifteen fathoms, and when it was towed through an un-seen shoal of herring, the bumps of the herring hitting the wire could be felt by the trained hand holding it. These touches revealed their presence. Of course, the length of the wire had to be varied constantly by the wireman, keeping it ideally within a few feet of the bottom. Too deep and you ran the risk of losing the lead on a rocky fastener; too high and it might pass over a shoal of bottom-hugging herring.

Wee Jamie would not entrust the vital jobs of either steering the boat or of holding the wire to anyone else. He stood outside the wheelhouse on the starboard side, his left arm steering through the open window, the wire held in his right hand. All around the starboard quarter of his boat *Irma*, the moulding iron (a metal strip which was fitted to the exposed edges of the wood in order to protect them) was almost cut through in a dozen places; scarred by the feeling wire's constant movement. These marks were looked at and spoken of with awe by us all – unique silent testimonials to the eccentric fishing skills of Wee Jamie

When echo sounders came into vogue, it was noticed that the ping emitting from the transmitter was audible to the human ear when the listener was, for example, in the fo'c's'le of a boat lying alongside the one whose sounder was running. Wee Jamie hearing this pronounced that 'them damn things'll jeest frighten aal the herrin' off the shore,' and for years refused to have one fitted. When eventually his son insisted on one being installed, it ran only when the son was on deck. As soon as he went below, off went the sounder!

Grieve Gemmell of Dunure told me that while still a young boy, fishing with his father Sammy, they passed inside the *Irma* and her neighbour the *Watercress*, who were lying off a bay to the north of Campbeltown one night. Seeing a small mark on the sounder, they shot and got about fifty baskets of good herring. The following morning, Grieve was on the pier in Campbeltown, listening to some local skippers discussing, as was their custom, the previous night's events.

'We were lyin' off Bobby's Rest,' piped up Wee Jamie indignantly in his soft Highland accent. 'We were lyin' there quietly listenin' tae a nice play o' herrin' getherin', when that bugger Gemmell cam' along wi' that sounder bang bangin' aweh, an' whoot he didna kill, he frightened!'

Grieve crept off quietly, before he was recognised.

My next port of call has to be Campbeltown. More of my Captains come from here because, having lived in the town, I knew more Campbeltonians than, for example, Carradale men.

The first of my Campbeltown Captains would seem to refute that statement, for I did not know Bobby 'The Hoodie' Robertson personally. I have heard and read a lot though, and just recently read an article describing him as having paved the way for the revolution in design of the entire Scottish fishing fleet.

He had several boats built, the best known of which were probably the *King-bird*, the *Kingfisher*, the *Kestrel*, and the *Kittiwake*, although a special place in the history books must be kept for the *Brothers*, the very first West Coast fishing boat, in 1907, to have an engine fitted. A book could be written about this extraordinary man, whose foresight and vision almost single-handedly dragged the fishing industry into the twentieth century. I do not think there will be any dissenting voices, particularly amongst readers of this book who are fishermen, if we promote him exclusively to Admiral. In any company anywhere, he could only be described as outstanding.

***Kingbird* leaving Peel**

Several contemporaries of The Hoodie must also be invited to join this exclusive Captaincy: John Short and John Wareham being the first; but we must not forget the Blair family who are credited in many quarters with doing more than any others to further the introduction of the ring net to the North, by their pioneering expeditions in their ringer the *Bengullion*. I have watched these men in their declining years set off on walks from the Weighus, at the head of the pier, away down the esplanade on the south side of the loch. What yarns must have been exchanged on these excursions. What would I give to be able to hear the reminiscences of such giants now?

The Weighus stood at the head of the Old Quay in Campbeltown. It was built to house the operators of the weighing machine which was used by carts, and latterly lorries which had been loaded from coasters berthed at the quay. On its wall was fixed a barometer which was consulted every day by the fishermen, but its presence provided shelter from the winds also, so it became a favourite stance for all the worthies of the day. It was removed to give greater vision to the drivers of the all-important motor car, when a roundabout was built to aid their passage.

My father was cook on board John Short's boat the *Kingbird* when she was new in the early 1930s (in fact I still have a piece of the ribbon from the bottle which launched her). He told me that one day when they were lying in Rothesay, mending a torn net, he approached the skipper and asked him for money to buy some meat for the dinner.

John, a small stocky character, was at an intricate part of the net-mending operation, and he answered in a preoccupied way, 'Ye'll no' need money boy, jeest tell the butcher who it's for. No, ye'll no' need money.' This was not a boastful proclamation, but a simple statement of fact. The names of such men were as good as hard cash, and their reputations were beyond reproach.

My father also told me that around this time the four Hoodie boats had been filled with herring in one night in the Kyles of Bute, had discharged them at Rothesay, gone back to sea, and had returned with three of them filled again – all within twenty four hours! I wonder how many herring could be caught there now?

John Wareham made a valiant attempt in the declining years of the ring-net fishings, to keep the two remaining boats, the *Kestrel* and the *Kittiwake*, at sea. Indeed it was said that he spent most of his personal savings in this attempt to help them survive, but in vain. The writing was on the wall by then. John was not happy unless he was at sea, and the patience displayed by such men in their pursuit of herring was phenomenal. This patience was not of course shared by all of the crew, and one bitterly cold February night when there was absolutely nothing being caught whilst the fleet was searching the Ballantrae Banks in the biting easterly wind, John's dogged persistence led to a famous incident with his crew.

They had watched the fleet gradually dwindle as other skippers gave up the fruitless search and made their way into Ayr harbour, and were understandably envious of the lucky crews of these boats who were by now sound asleep in their warm bunks.

Soon they and their neighbour were the only boats left on the sea. John in the wheelhouse regularly asked the poor man who was slowly freezing as he held the feeling wire which trailed astern, 'Are ye feelin' anything?'

Eventually this poor man got hold of a broom and fixed it upright into the aft part of the boat and draped his oilskin over it. He fixed his sou'wester above this, and sneaked below to the blessed heat of the engine room where he promptly fell asleep. It was not until daylight started to come in that John realised the reason for the silence which had greeted all of his questions – there was no one there feeling for the herring! The squeals of temper which accompanied this discovery were spoken of in awe for years.

'Baldy' Stewart was another whose name should be written large in the annals of the fishing industry. A short pipe-smoking barrel of a man always ready to smile and crack a joke, his jovial face will live forever in the memories of all who knew him. For many years he skippered the *Boy Danny* successfully, and my most enduring memory of him also reflects the generally high standard of feeling evident in these days for one's fellow fishermen, which has now apparently been eroded beyond recall. This event occurred at the Manx fishing, when the herring were invariably caught south and west of Peel. No one looked on the east side of the island at all.

The fleet was in Peel one morning after a night which had produced very light returns, when the word got out that Baldy was in Portpatrick with a big shot of herring. No one knew where he had caught them, no one had seen the lucky pair during the previous night's fishing, so speculation was rife on the quay. Telephone calls to the fish salesman's office in Portpatrick revealed only that the fortunate crews had been sworn to secrecy, but eventually Baldy himself came to the telephone and told his tormentors that he would reveal the secret on the radio that afternoon whilst on his way back to the grounds. Keeping the secret until then meant that he would be in a position to compete equally with the rest of the fleet that coming night.

At the appointed hour he came on the radio and revealed to all that the herring had been killed off Douglas, on the east side of the island. Baldy did not want his competitors to get an advantage over him, but he was not prepared to tell lies to preserve his position.

I remember a similar occasion, but on a much smaller scale, involving myself. We were fishing one Friday in the Minch in June, and got a small but valuable shot at Muldonich Island at the mouth of Castlebay, whilst very little was being caught among the rest of the fleet. On the way into Mallaig we were all told that we must not disclose to anyone just where we had got them.

On taking the hatches off in Mallaig we discovered a smallish salmon lying on top of the catch. It had been brailed aboard with the herring, unseen by anyone. I was on the quay prior to starting to discharge the catch, when I was approached by 'Uncle' Jimmy Sloan, another immortal (of whom more later). He approached, pipe as usual in the corner of his mouth, and inquired of me, in a conspiratorial tone, just where we had got the herring.

'Baldy' Stewart
(Susan Hughan)

Now Uncle Jimmy was a man of whom mere mortals stood in awe – especially young lads like the one from whom he was now trying to elicit information – and I was finding it very difficult indeed to withstand his intense questioning. Suddenly I remembered the salmon.

'Come here and see what we found on top of the herring when we took the hatches off this morning Uncle Jimmy,' I said, in a forlorn attempt to buy time, leading him to the edge of the quay from where he could look down into the open hold. I pointed at the salmon.

'Aw, that's a richt bonny fish boy,' said Uncle Jimmy. 'Whaur did ye get it?'

I very nearly told him!

To return to Baldy. He retired from the fishing and lived in a wee flat at the head of the New Quay, alone except for his constant companion, a little terrier dog. He must have been in his seventies when he went to Rothesay on a motor yacht, the *Quesada*, taking his dog with him of course.

On the return trip, the weather deteriorated very quickly. The *Quesada* got into difficulties right at the mouth of Campbeltown Loch and sank, taking with her several young men. Incredibly, Baldy not only got out of her safely, but took his beloved dog with him!

His son Willie, 'Suet' to all, unfortunately died as this book was being written. Willie was another kind and gentle man who is remembered with delight by me, and I am certain by all of his contemporaries. He had been a Lieutenant Commander in the Royal Navy during the war, and one result of his being in the Officers' mess was that on the odd occasion when he took a wee dram, his speech became more 'proper' than normal. So the theory went anyway! One thing for sure, I don't think that anyone ever heard him use foul or profane language at any time, no matter what the circumstances were.

I will never forget him one night in Lochboisdale aboard the *Golden Hind* when there was an impromptu concert in full swing. His turn to sing came around – no-one was excused this duty – so he reluctantly got to his feet. 'I cannot sing at all well, so I will recite a poetry.'

He began:

> *Little spider on the wall, You ain't got no hair at all.*
> *You ain't got a comb to comb your hair*
> *But you don't care 'Cos you ain't got no hair!*

The 'poem' concluded, Willie subsided slowly back to his previous relaxed position by the table, a beatific smile on his face all the while.

Jock Meenan was another contemporary of Baldy's, and for many years he skippered the *Stella Maris*. He was a tall austere man, who thought more than he talked. His son and daughter emigrated to America while still quite young, and it was a great surprise to all when Jock and his wife followed, leaving his nephew Jim in charge of the boat.

Jock Meenan

43

Cecil Finn, who served his time with Jock, and who shared my admiration for the man, told me that most of Jock's time in America was spent watching men sail model yachts in a pond near his new home, which was many miles from the sea. In due course he and his wife flew back to Scotland on holiday, completing the final leg of the trip to Campbeltown aboard one of the Clyde steamers. En route, the steamer called at Lochranza, where Jock spotted his beloved *Stella Maris* at anchor in the bay. Bribing a small boy to row him out to her, he left the steamer there and then and didn't see his wife again until the end of the week!

'Captain' Jock was a sore loss to the fishing community in Campbeltown, but Jim Meenan, his nephew, having donned the vacant mantle, wore it with distinction for not nearly enough years. I must be counted among the many who had a great regard for Jim – he who never seemed to see the dark side of anyone's nature – and remember one day being horrified when he said that another fisherman was in his opinion 'not very intelligent, but possessing a vast amount of low animal cunning, which is much more important!' I initially thought that this was a derogatory remark – which would have been completely out of character from Jim – but since then of course I have realised that he was in fact being complimentary to the man.

Jim was skipper of the *Stella Maris* when the stakes became higher, but he never sacrificed integrity at the altar of money, and the loss to the industry was great indeed when he died very young. Shortly after his death I was in Glasgow, and booked into the Loretto Hotel. This hotel – now closed and the owner dead – drew most of its guests from the West Coast, with Campbeltown and Mallaig featuring often in the pages of the Visitors' Book, and it was rare indeed to stay there without meeting a weel-kent face. When I arrived I was subjected to the usual interrogation about the latest gossip, by the owner Angus Campbell, and I asked him if he had known Jim Meenan. 'Yes of course,' was his reply, but when I told Angus that Jim had just died, he startled me by turning on his heels and walking quickly away. My puzzlement was resolved when he returned to my room later, and in some distress suggested that when I left, I should not pay him, but use the money I owed to him to buy some flowers for Jim's widow! As I was not likely to be in Campbeltown for some time I convinced him that this was not a good idea, and I do not know the ultimate outcome, but it does illustrate the high regard in which Jim was held by even casual acquaintances.

In the days when medium frequency radio was the only means of communicating with one's neighbour when, for example, you were on way back from market, it was often difficult to get through the crowded airwaves, so a series of whistles were used by the callers to identify themselves. These whistled tunes would be heard through the most crowded traffic, and meant that the listeners should go to another less crowded prearranged frequency. Jim always used 'Eileen Allanah'. I never hear this tune without thinking of him, and I often wonder if these transmissions are still winging their way through eternal space.

Robert McGown of the *Felicia* was another dedicated man whose integrity was greatly admired by those less gifted. In common with many of the others he did not drink alcohol at all, and his weekly treat was to buy a half pound of peppermints on a Saturday, so Angus will have to supply something other than whisky for a great many of my Captains!

Moving on to a younger generation, no mention of Campbeltown fishermen would be complete without reference to Duncan Macdonald, better known as 'Dunky Donal', who skippered the *Golden Hind*. The last time I met him, he had a small boy by the hand. In response to the prompt, 'Tell this man what your name is,' the lad replied in a loud voice 'Dunky Donal!' The delight on Dunky senior's face, on hearing his grandson lay claim to the name, was something to see.

I first became aware of Dunky before I left school, when he was aboard my father's boat, the *Golden Fleece*. He was a big genial man, a bluff happy character who was, when excited, inclined to stutter slightly. He laughed a lot, but was reputedly not too happy in the dark.

The story was told to me of the time when the boat was lying in Port St Mary on the Isle of Man, waiting for a lull in the weather. In due course, the wind went up to the west, and eased. This abatement was accompanied by a very heavy downpour. The crew had all, with the exception of Dunky, come back aboard before the rain started, but the cook, 'Wee Mo' – this because of his lack of stature – was sent to fetch the missing Dunky.

Mo donned an almost white raincoat belonging to my father which, as it was much too big for him, he pulled over his head, and set off up the south side of the street. He had not gone very far when, through the murky darkness of the night, he saw the figure of a man on the north side of the street, head down against the rain, going toward the pier.

Mo stopped, not at all sure of the identity of the man, but eventually, after he had passed, decided that it was indeed the person for whom he was searching, so he set off in pursuit. Dunky, for his part, became aware only of a ghostly white figure behind him, convinced himself correctly that this apparition was chasing him, so he set off at a rapid rate of knots down the pier, calling for assistance as he neared the boat! To his eternal credit, he delighted in telling this story against himself.

The *Golden Hind*, which Dunky later bought, was a large, very powerful boat for her day. She was fitted with a Kelvin diesel, of an almost unheard of 132 horse power. This of course made her very fast in comparison with her companions, and Dunky was very proud of the vessel's speed and manoeuvrability. One dark January night, Dunky had the misfortune to strike the outside edge of the Stuleys, a small group of unlit islands off the east coast of South Uist. The damage was all underwater, so it was not possible to see just what repairs were necessary, but it was agreed that we in the *Golden Fleece* should escort him to Mallaig where expert help was available.

Dunky's boat, despite its disability, was still very much faster than ours, so we arrived some time after he had beached the *Golden Hind* in Mallaig. When the tide had fallen enough, Charlie Henderson the local boatbuilder appeared on the scene, and accompanied by an anxious Dunky, proceeded to survey the damage.

'What sort of speed were you doing?' was Charlie's first question.

'Full bit,' replied Dunky tremulously, fearing the worst. A long pause followed, with Charlie prodding the injured forefoot. Eventually he spoke.

'Ye've hurt her dignity, Dunky,' he said quietly.

The roars from the relieved Dunky could be heard miles away.

'Hear that,' he bellowed to all and sundry. 'Full bore on tae the Stuleys, an' aal I did was hurt her dignity. Some ship this, eh!'

Dunky was enjoying a very successful spell of fishing in the Mull lochs, landing good shots of herring into Oban almost every day, when the dreadful disease *Myxomatosis* was introduced to the rabbit population and was headline news in most newspapers. It had also become his habit to have a wee dram in one of the local hostelries on occasion. One day not long after he had come into the bar, he slid onto the floor, his feet waving wildly in the air.

'What's wrong wi' ye, Dunky?' shouted the thoroughly alarmed barman.

'Ah've got *mix ma toes*,' was the reply from the irrepressible Dunky!

The Minch fishing subjected all its participants to long spells of boredom, cooped up in what can only be described as abysmal conditions, when bad weather confined them to anchor in some remote loch. This boredom was relieved in many ways. For example, one game of 'I spy' aboard the *Golden Hind* ended in complete confusion when a glorious character who rejoiced in the nickname of 'Neep', had them all baffled with the initials LL. When at last they had all given in, Neep revealed that it meant 'Lectric Light', and promptly got severely thumped for his lack of spelling ability!

There was however one unique event devised by Dunky and his crew. They would perform a play! The opening night arrived, and the show was a sell-out. The audience filled the fo'c's'le entirely, and the unfortunates who could not be accommodated below decks tried to view the fun by looking through the open skylight, from the foredeck. I do not know who was responsible for the script, but the show went thus:

Actor No.1 is seen sweeping the yard at his home in the deep south of America (actually the forecastle of the *Golden Hind*).

Actor No.2 appears slowly from the hold lazily carrying a rifle (formerly a broom handle), and greets No.1 thus:

'Howdy, Paw.'

'Howdy, Son.' is the reply, in a drawling Southern American accent gleaned from the cinema but redolent of Campbeltown. 'Where ya bin, Son?'

'Ah've bin to the war, Paw.'

'What'd ya do in the war, Son?'

'Ah done a heap a killin', Paw.'

'What ya do ya killin' with, Son?'

'Ah done a heap a killin' wi' ma ol' rifle, Paw' (this said brandishing the broom handle), 'an' ah done a heap a killin' wi' ma pineapples too.'

'Pineapples, Son, what's pineapples?'

'This here's a pineapple, Paw,' says the son (brandishing a large potato from which protrudes a match). 'See that there li'l' green shed, Paw? Well, watch this!'

The actor playing the part of the son then pulls the match from the potato with his teeth, counts to five, and throws it into a bunk. This is the signal for everyone to make as much noise as possible, and for lights to be flashed on and off simulating an explosion.

'That sure is a mighty pow'ful weapon, Son,' says Paw, when the noise dies down. 'Ya shouldn' ha' done that though.'

'Why not Paw?'

'Because yore Maw was in that li'l' green shed, Son!'

Dunky was a successful fisherman, very popular with his fellows from all over Scotland, and is certainly a Captain who would be welcome at any fireside.

Henry Martin
(Susan Hughan)

47

5

A great many of the happier memories of my early days at the fishing are centred around the Isle of Man, with its west coast port of Peel a favourite among us all. There was a legend there that the Manx people always ate their meat before their soup, in order to thwart the hungry thieving Scottish marauders who, in the old days, raided and pillaged there, but they always made us very welcome.

I remember sitting in a group above the harbour at Peel one fine summer day, when two old ladies stopped to view the fleet of boats assembled there.

'What do these letters on the boats mean?' asked one of them, referring to the registration marks which were painted on the bow and stern of each ringer.

'CN, my dear, stands for Campbeltown,' answered James McNaughton, better known as 'Madrala', and another well-loved shipmate of mine. 'BA means Ballantrae, and PL is for Peel.'

'How interesting!' replied one of the ladies, 'And what does KY signify?' – this said pointing to one of the boats from the Firth of Forth, which was registered at Kirkcaldy.

'That means that this boat is from Kentucky,' offered the irrepressible Madrala, and off went the old dears, marvelling at the distances travelled in the pursuit of herring!

As young men who had, in common with most other young men, a mistaken idea of their own abilities, we raised the dust in most of the many ports of call, but in the Isle of Man we always walked just a little bit smaller.

A few years ago, my wife and I enjoyed a visit from a Manx lady and her husband, who had been friends of mine in those blithe days, and during our recollections of the happy hours spent dancing in the small village dance-hall in Peel, this lady suddenly asked me if I remembered a fight taking place there. Thinking that she was referring to an incident which I had forgotten, I questioned her for more details.

'Oh no,' she replied, 'I am not referring to a specific fight, I am asking if you remember there *ever* being an occasion when one took place?' I couldn't, but since then I have become aware of one of the reasons why.

We were afraid of the consequences of being arrested. Not, I hasten to add, afraid of the Manx Police who were very fair, but no matter how tough we thought we might be, the threat of possibly being sentenced to having our trousers taken down and being birched made us think twice before offering violence to anyone. What say your so-called Civil Rights workers to that?

At the Peel dances there was always an interval during which the band went

At the Peel dances there was always an interval during which the band went to the nearest hotel for a drink. I remember one night a conga started up during this interval, and – led by one glorious character who must remain nameless – it wound its way out of the hall, went all the way along the promenade and back again to the hall, increasing in size by the minute... with never a cross word being exchanged.

Whitby, too, brings fond memories, and one night about five years ago, I had a good laugh about those days. I was in the Marine Hotel in Mallaig, in the company of two Lifeboat Inspectors. It was winter and the hotel was quiet, so we asked the only other occupants of the cocktail bar to join our company. The young couple were English, and when I discovered that the girl hailed from Whitby, I exclaimed 'Whitby! Why that is where I spent many happy days when I was young. I used to fish for herring from that port many years ago.' On hearing this, the girl, in a rather agitated manner, demanded to see my hands! I hesitantly held them out palm upward, whereupon she said excitedly, 'No, I want to see the backs of them!' When I had turned them over for her inspection, wondering just what was going on, she then said in a disappointed tone, 'No, it's not you, I'm afraid.'

Her husband laughingly explained that she was always on the lookout for her father, who had been a Scottish fisherman, and the only thing her mother could remember about him was that she thought he had a knuckle missing on one of his hands! Now if anyone reading this. . .!

I fear that I have strayed too long from the company of Captains, so must return, and in returning, move a little closer to the present day scene in Campbeltown before moving on to other places .

Neil Speed was skipper of the *Moira*, one of the more modern and larger ringers. He was a very well turned out man, always trim, dapper and smart-looking, with a military bearing. He smoked a pipe almost incessantly, and was another who was lost to us tragically much too young, leaving his son, also named Neil, to carry on the job.

An award for bravery during the war had been deservedly won by him, but in common with his fellows, when he spoke of that dark period his tales were all light-hearted ones. Some time after his death I went into the shop where his widow worked. I had been at the library, and was on my way home with my books which I casually laid on the counter.

Mrs Speed idly picked them up, and saw that one of them was about Captain Walker, RN, a brilliant officer who revolutionised the war against the U-boats in the Atlantic, and who almost certainly killed himself with overwork in the process of defeating them. He was also renowned for not suffering fools gladly, a fact commented upon in several of the books written about him after his death.

Mrs Speed told me that Neil had been drafted to Captain Walker's ship as

Coxswain (the Coxswain of a Royal Navy ship is the senior rating aboard, and holds an extremely responsible job). It was made very plain to Neil, by Walker, that he was not too happy at being sent a 'hostilities only' man for this post. That Neil had been a fisherman before the war seemed to reduce his chances of being accepted by Captain Walker, but he was assured that he would be given a fair chance to prove his worth. He succeeded in gaining the confidence of his commanding officer and served with him for over a year. On being drafted to another ship, he was invited into Walker's cabin on the morning of his departure. There two glasses of whisky were poured, and the two men toasted one another's health. Neil asked for, and was given the glass from which his CO had drunk.

This glass, I was told, had pride of place in the china cabinet in Neil's home. No-one was allowed to touch it, but Neil took it out at midnight every Hogmanay, filled it with whisky, drank to 'absent friends', and put it back unwashed – as indeed it had remained since his old boss 'Johnnie' Walker had drunk from it so many years before. Neil has rejoined his old ship now. I bet the yarn was good when they met again!

There are of course current contenders for Captaincy among the fishermen of the 'Wee Toon'. One of the leaders of the pack must be Cecil Finn, my childhood pal, and owner of the *Brighter Morn*, whose apprenticeship started so long ago in Brown's house. He is semi-retired now, but plays a very active part in the political scene, which has become so important nowadays, and since I started writing this epistle, he has been honoured by being awarded the MBE for his work in this field. He is the same age as me, is sturdily built, and until time demanded its toll, he sported a shock of red hair. He closely resembles Amos of *Emmerdale Farm*. Oddly enough he and I married girls with the same Christian names.

He used a pipe until recently. I say 'used', advisedly. It had become a prop which helped to delay answers to questions which require a bit of thought, but like other stratagems have in the past, so this one backfired on him on one occasion not too long ago. Literally!

I am told, by someone who was there, that Cecil had been despatched by his colleagues to 'sort out' the Navy, who had announced to the fishermen that they required a piece of water in the Clyde in which to hold a mine-sweeping exercise, and that the local fishermen should keep well away from this area while the exercise took place. This piece of water was a prime fishing area, and it was felt among the fishing community that the Navy should go elsewhere to play their games.

On this sorting out errand he was accompanied by a cousin of mine, Robert 'Trapper' Gillies, who is another obvious contender for Captaincy. Robert, with his brother Willie, fishes the *Nova Spero*. The delegation was completed by the inclusion of Patrick Stewart – a lawyer, and the third generation of his family to hold the post of Secretary to the Clyde Fishermen's Association.

When they arrived at the Naval base they were greeted by a 'Four-Ringer' and his staff, who had all been to the Naval charm school, which teaches its amounts of high-proof gin. The hospitality which they dispensed was being accepted gratefully by all except Patrick, who abstained from partaking of the good spirits on the grounds that he had to drive the others home. When the Naval contingent, experts at the art, decided that the time was right, a chart of the Clyde was spread over the table and the sales pitch began!

'Now then gentlemen, we intend laying our mines heah, heah, and heah, which I am sure you will agree won't affect your fishing efforts at all, don't you see?'

Thus began the aristocratic leader of the Naval hosts. Our two candidates, when they tried to focus on the areas indicated by the pointer wielded by the Captain, realised that they had underestimated the potency of the duty-free gin, and Cecil, in order to gain time, produced his pipe and started to apply lit matches to it, sucking noisily as he did so. Trapper, however, lacking such a prop, viewed the chart through the haze (only part of which came from Cecil's pipe), then grabbed the distinguished Naval personage by the lapels, and stated in his usual very loud, very Campbeltown accent, 'Aye, that's aa' right Jeck, but whoot if they pit thim in the wrang place!'

Cecil was by now very agitated, an observation borne out by the fact that he was still applying lit matches to his pipe although there were actually flames coming from the bowl! The Naval person, not at all happy at being grabbed in this manner, shook himself free and in a very hurt tone declared, 'That won't happen, my officahs are all highly trained navigatahs.'

Trapper re-attached himself to the Captain's lapels and roared up at him, 'Aye, Jeck, but whoot if they're a' full o' gin, eh?'

As this riposte registered in Cecil's brain, he snorted!

Burning tobacco was blown all over the chart, causing countless fires to break out all over it and the table, and the meeting broke up in total confusion!

What cousin Trapper lacks in stature he more than makes up for in volume, and his habit of referring to all – close friend or stranger; male or female – as 'Jeck', has led to some confusion at times. His use of this mode of address caused a great deal of consternation in a young lady, highly literate in several languages, who was serving as interpreter to him in Brussels on one occasion. Having listened to Robert in full flight for some time, she felt moved to ask in a most plaintive voice, 'Excuse please, what means this Jeck?'

Cecil told me that once, during a holiday in Tenerife, he had been brought up 'all standing', by local fishermen. He had made contact with them socially and was aware that they used nets similar to ring-nets, with which they caught anchovies. He was also aware that they did not have even the most basic kind of echo sounder on their boats. Seeking to assist them, yet trying his best not to be patronising, he tentatively brought up the subject of fish-finding, and told them

c1950 aboard the *Stella Maris* in Moonen Bay, Skye
(l-r): Duncan McIsaac, John Meenan, Cecil Finn, James Meenan, Dennis Meenan

that their Scottish counterparts used an electronic device to help them catch herring (which have habits similar to those of the anchovy). When asked if he still used a ring-net to kill herring, he replied in the negative, saying that there was currently a five-year ban on herring catching, in an attempt to preserve the sorely depleted stocks.

His single-minded attempt to bring these men into the twentieth century came to an abrupt halt when they replied, 'No, we will not have this machine. We will keep our anchovies!'

Cecil and Robert are successful fishermen who have also succeeded in gaining respect from their fellows; not an easy task nowadays. During the time when herring was the prey, it was not uncommon for crews to go without wages for several weeks at a time; and this was accepted by all, simply because there was the chance to make enough in one lucky night to make up for the lean weeks.

This is not the case now. There is no opportunity to make a quick killing, so it has become one long slog for all concerned. Every day must be made to count, and the resultant pressures of trying to overcome all of the natural obstacles have been compounded by the seemingly impossible task of trying to adhere to the oft-times crazy legislation imposed by the bureaucrats, who in the main know nothing of the industry which they are trying to regulate.

One fisherman commented to me: 'When I started fishing, I fished where I wanted to, when I wanted to, for what I thought I could sell. Now I have a bit of paper which allows me to fish in certain places, at stated times, for specific types of fish – and I'm desperately trying to hold on to that!'

The pressure which has been imposed upon men who are already under stress from natural causes, has led to many of them straying from the designated paths of legality, and in so doing being branded as criminals, when all they want to do is to get on with the job in hand, and make a living for their families. If possible, it is much better to laugh at the results of such 'crimes', and indeed some of them are comical.

Whilst fishing for sprats in the upper limits of the Clyde, one pair who shall remain nameless, took a good haul of large herring. Lucky? Well, no! The herring season was over, and to land these herring – which incidentally were now dead – was illegal. By law, they should have been dumped! Our heroes were not prepared to do this, however; so after a few telephone calls they betook themselves, loaded with herring, to a disused pier in one of the lochs nearby. In due course, two articulated lorries arrived to take the herring to a processing factory. As the road to the pier was too narrow to accommodate these lorries, a small truck was commissioned to ferry the catch to them. This operation was well under way, when one of the local householders who was by now thoroughly alarmed by this unusual nocturnal activity, telephoned the police.

Picture the scene: A boat is discharging an 'illegal' cargo in a pitch dark, remote Scottish loch. Everyone involved is tense and apprehensive. Suddenly, through the trees which line the approach road to the pier, there appears the blue flashing light of a police car! It was some time before the police decided that this activity did not warrant any more investigation, and left, weighted down with fries of herring. All fears of a holiday in Barlinnie dispelled, the shattered crews were able to continue their toil unhindered!

The same pair had a similar catch aboard on another dark night, and it was decided that a furtive visit to Campbeltown was needed to arrange for the disposal of the illegal cargo. The skipper of one of the boats went to bed for some much-needed sleep, and left his brother with the insufficient instructions, 'Away ye go for Campbeltown.' Imagine the scene when, awakened by the sound of the boat going astern, he came on deck to find that his unsuspecting brother had tied up alongside the Fishery Protection Vessel at Campbeltown Quay!

On a slightly different tack, I heard a lovely, though thoroughly alarming, story of a Rothesay man who got himself into serious trouble when on a salmon poaching expedition.

There is apparently a very good salmon river in the Kyles of Bute, which is a great attraction to those who enjoy a night at such sport. However, anyone leaving Rothesay on a summer evening and heading west in a motor boat was inevitably seen. Their intentions were readily realised, and they ran the risk of having a reception committee awaiting them on their arrival at the river. Our hero had hit on the ploy of leaving in a rowing boat, reckoning that no one would suspect that a potential poacher would dream of undertaking to row the considerable distance to the river. As an accomplice he chose one – let us call him 'Dougie' – who was renowned for his strength, but not for his mental abilities. We should also refer to the prime subject in this yarn as 'Willie'.

This intrepid pair rowed for miles, until nearing the river and hearing a fish jump close to the shore, they quietly rowed in and shot their net – which was about a hundred yards long – from the shore out in a semi-circle around the area in which the fish had jumped, then back to the shore. This effort unfortunately drew a blank, but they decided that they should have a cup of tea from the flasks which they each had taken with them. In the landing of these flasks, Dougie's was dropped by Willie and, of course, broke.

Dougie blew his top about this in no uncertain terms and accused Willie of dropping it on purpose. He refused to take the proffered share of Willie's flask, and announced that in reprisal for what he saw as an act of vandalism against him, he would not now row the boat any further. Willie therefore rowed the remaining short distance to the river by himself, but on reaching it, broke the uneasy silence to ask Dougie to row across the river mouth whilst he, Willie, shot the net. This was reluctantly agreed, the dinghy was slowly backed into one side of the river bank, a heavy stone with the end of the net attached was thrown ashore, and the slow silent shooting process was begun.

Less than half way through this action, Willie was startled to see through the gloaming a bailiff run down the beach, grab the end of the net and start hauling it ashore. Seeing that the bailiff was alone, Willie stood on the net remaining in the

54

boat – which meant that they were now being drawn toward the shore – and, seeking to dissuade the man from hauling, he roared 'Now then *Jimmy,* there's only one of them. As soon as we hit the shore, brain him with an oar!'

The bailiff, however, was made of stern stuff and continued pulling the net, and Willie was mortified when – as soon as the boat's keel touched bottom – Dougie vaulted past him and felled the hapless man with a blow to the head from the oar.

'Ye telt me tae dae it,' was the uncaring response from Dougie, when the horrified Willie suggested that the man had been killed and asked what on earth they could do now.

'So jeest roll his body intae the watter. Naebody'll ever ken what happened!'

Willie examined the poor man and, deciding that there was no lasting damage done, he started to bathe his bleeding wound. Seeing the first feeble signs of recovery he told Dougie to gather up the net into the boat, and to be prepared to row for his life. The casualty was now responding sensibly to questions, and the indications were that his next step would be to open his eyes, so recognising this, Willie stood up and shouted loudly, 'Row *Jimmy* row. Back tae *Tarbert* as fast as ye can!'

'No way, Willie! Tae Hell wi' rowin' tae Tarbert,' Dougie yelled in return. 'I'm gaun back tae Rothesay where we came from!' It would be better to draw a veil over the rest of this sorry saga.

I would not be forgiven if I left Campbeltown without mention of my father. He was demobbed from the Navy in 1945, and shortly afterwards bought a second-hand boat to pursue the career he loved, hunting herring. With hindsight, the boat which he bought was too small and too old. It was also bought at a time when boats were commanding a very high price, sought after by many young men returning from the war who wanted to get a share of the good fishings which had prevailed whilst they were away. That he succeeded in being among the best earners for a number of years, despite the handicap of trying to keep up with bigger boats, is a measure of the man.

He also died young, as a result of a drowning accident, and his popularity among his fellow fishermen was well illustrated by the number who travelled long distances to pay their last respects at his funeral.

One year, around Christmas, he bought a Labrador pup in Lochboisdale and, immediately after the purchase had been completed, this poor wee animal was subjected, on a poor night, to the horrors of crossing the Minch, en route to Campbeltown. It was sick as a dog!

My young brother was still at school then and, as fishermen, my father and I were away from home for probably nine months of the year. Despite the fact that my brother took care of the dog, and my mother fed him, there was no mistaking who was his master. As soon as my father came home, Glen, for that was his name, went wherever he went. We often saw the poor dog sitting outside whichever pub my father had chosen to indulge in his great weakness for whisky, but Glen refused to abandon his vigil for any of us. His name was heard often aboard the boat, for whenever anyone made a mistake of any kind, the roar would arise from my father, 'My Glen could do better than that!'

He was never happier than when among herring, and when it became obvious that the days of the ring-net were over he, like so many others, was unable to put his heart into fishing for any other species.

On one occasion, my mother refused to accompany my father to the annual Fishermen's Ball, until he had promised that he would drink only lager. The hall in which this Ball was held adjoined the Royal Hotel, a favourite haunt of his, so he had the barman well primed that whenever he asked for a lager, the barman would surreptitiously add a gill of whisky to it! All went well – he was getting his dram – and my mother was happy that he was drinking only lager, until a friend, who was 'feeling no pain', insisted that he would buy my father a drink. He was surprised to be handed a glass of lager when he had demanded 'a dram for Tommy', but when the barman asked him for money far in excess of the expected price of the lager, his surprise exploded into voluble anger. This of course let the cat out of the bag, and meant an end to that little ploy!

I leave Campbeltown with a poem written, I have been told, by a schoolgirl whose surname was McNiven, and which was published in the *Campbeltown Courier* many years ago. It contains the names of many of the old ringers, and was taught to me by my mother.

> The *King Bird* fled with the *Fairy Queen* into the *Golden Dawn.*
> The *Marie Stella* watched their flight, but the rest of the world slept on.
> The *Busy Bee* was the first to awake, so she went to the *Mystical Rose.*
> 'They have gone,' she cried, 'What can we do, perhaps *Bengullion* knows.'
> 'Let the *Frigate Bird* pursue,' he cried, 'In her garb of *Silver Grey.*'
> And *Swift* as the *Crimson Arrow* sped the beautiful ship away.
> Then the *Blue Bird* cried, 'I am as *Swift* as light, *Nulli Secundus* am I,
> I will bring them back, or return no more.' And the *Falcon* made reply,
> '*Nil Desperandum*, I will go forth on this *Enterprise* with you.'
> But the goddess *Felicia* shook her head, and helped the lovers through.
> So they came no more to their old *Sweet Home*, where the *Kingfisher* roams at will
> But *Ave Maria's* sweet notes recall the Loch they both love still

6

Across the Firth of Clyde, on the Ayrshire coast, were fishermen of like minds and spirits to the ones we have been meeting, and it is to there that I now turn to find my next quorum of Captains.

The first village on our journey south from Ayr is Dunure, a small community living in neat houses which cling to the rocky slopes leading to the tiny harbour. There lived one of the most extraordinary of my candidates – Sammy Gemmell of the *Storm Drift*.

One of five sea-going brothers, Sammy was not a very tall man, but he carried a lot of weight around his middle. His opinions also carried a great deal of weight with his fellow fishermen. He was a very successful skipper, but was also probably unique in that he was both a politician and an honest man. These two descriptions are usually a contradiction in terms in my estimation.

He started his political career early, after one very hard week when the herring which he had succeeded in catching had been more than usually difficult to sell. It was then common practice that bribes be given to buyers as an incentive for them to buy the herring, but this had got completely out of hand (as is common with all such devices), and it was not unknown for the fishermen, desperate to market their hard-won catches, to give away half of the shot.

Sammy Gemmell

Sammy went home one Saturday and, on reviewing the past week's work, became aware that he had given his crew ten shillings (50p) as their share of the earnings, but had given a buyer three pounds nine shillings (£3:45p), for his 'graft'. This horrified him as much as it should horrify you, but Sammy took steps which no one had taken before, and which I cannot see anyone else taking now.

This bribery, although common practice, was outwith the rules which the Clyde Fishermen's Association had written to govern themselves, so he took himself to the then Chairman of the Association and turned himself in, demanding to know how he was to be punished. The man unsurprisingly did not know how to handle this situation, so Sammy in desperation went to Campbeltown where he confessed all to Archibald Stewart, the afore-mentioned lawyer, and Secretary of the Association.

The ensuing discussion between the two of them took up many hours, and resulted in the starting of a pooling agreement, which briefly meant that the prices of comparably sized and quality herring were pooled, an average was worked out, and this average price was paid to all participants. The pooling system meant, of course, that there was no longer any gain for those indulging in bribery, and its continued use today is a lasting memorial to Sammy Gemmell.

Sammy was given a gold watch by his grateful fellow-fishermen from Whitby in an unprecedented gesture of thanks for his help to them, and it was a favourite prank of his to use this watch – which was waterproof – to stir his tea. This was usually done when he had partaken of a few drams, and caused great consternation amongst many.

While in the chair at a meeting of fishermen with the Herring Industry Board, Sammy took exception to the long-winded speech being given by Sir Frederick Bell, who was at that time Chairman of the Board. He stood up and told Sir Frederick to 'Sit on your arse and shut up. You hav'na' got it in ye tae be a fisherman onywey!' I am reliably assured that Sir Frederick wisely followed this advice!

Ian Stewart, the lawyer who succeeded his father, Archibald, as Secretary to the Fishermen's Association, told me that Sammy – who did not suffer fools gladly – on one occasion told another prominent politician who was running off at the mouth, to 'Sit doon an' stop speakin' a lot o' soft shite!' He served as Chairman of the Clyde Fishermen's Association with great distinction for four years, and when he retired was deservedly awarded the MBE by the Queen for his services to a grateful fishing community.

When his successors recently went to London to protest to the Government about the killing of the crew of the *Antares* by a submarine, to my absolute amazement they took with them samples of their produce which they handed in to Downing Street. I have no idea of what Sammy would have done in the same sad circumstances, but he most assuredly would not have gone bearing gifts. The industry could use a man of his stature now, to lead it out of the mess it is in!

His son, Grieve, took over the reins from Sammy in the 1960s and continued the successful fishing side of the Gemmell saga. Grieve is very well known and liked among fishermen everywhere, and was probably the last of the ring-net exponents to make a good living at the winter fishing in the Minch.

On a recent visit to Dunure he told me, whilst reminiscing, that his first trip as a fisherman had been through the Forth and Clyde Canal to fish herring into Anstruther. This was in 1940, not long after war had started. They fished there for only three weeks, then left because acoustic mines had been laid around the area in which they had been working, and he thought that the accidental detonation of some of these mines – whilst not resulting in loss of life – had caused injuries to some of the fishermen. They were there for three weeks, and earned just over £300 each for the trip. Big money indeed in those far off days!

He was there when the big steel purse-seiners arrived on the scene and he recognised with so many others that they would destroy the old ways. I heard him on the pier in Mallaig telling a group, which included purse-seine skippers, that he had been at the boatbuilder in Girvan on his weekend at home.

Asked if he was building a new boat, he replied with his usual pawkish humour. 'No, Ah wis lukkin' fur a big weldin' machine tae weld a' they tin pursers together, so they couldna' get oot!'

He also said to me on one occasion, 'There's nae herm in a bottle o' whisky. No. As lang as ye keep it in the bottle, there's nae herm in it. It's when ye let it oot o' the bottle that the trouble starts!'

He has a great regard for his fellow creatures of the Earth. It was common for seagulls to have their feathers completely soaked whilst they were trying to feed from the bag of herring in a ring-net. The oil from the herring destroyed the waterproofing on their feathers and the poor gulls would not float at their designed waterline, and so ran the serious risk of being drowned! On one occasion in Shepherds Bight, Grieve had the wheelhouse almost filled with rescued gulls, and he refused to leave for the market until they had all dried off properly. His neighbour, also filled with herring, left immediately. The wind was just about gale force and the boat which had left early had an extremely bad crossing, but by the time the gulls had dried off, the wind had eased and Grieve, he told me, had a relatively good passage.

Their last winter in the Minch gave them good fishings, and early in the season they were lying in Mallaig harbour waiting to discharge their catch when Grieve's attention was drawn to a cat trapped under the pier, and which was about to be drowned by the rapidly rising tide. He rescued this poor animal, and not only saw that it was fed every day that they were in Mallaig, but when leaving for home, told the oil merchant that he must feed the cat for as long as was necessary. The bill for the food was to be sent to him!

The engine room of the *Storm Drift* was absolutely immaculate – the cleanest by far that I have ever seen anywhere. Its gleaming brightness was not surpassed by any yacht I have ever been aboard, and it was certainly an enormous tribute to the hard work put into it by the engineer Davie Edgar, better known to us all as 'Horsey' who sadly lost a son to the sea very recently. The price of fish!

59

When I last met Grieve, I asked him what he was doing to pass the time. He told me, then added, 'Some mornin's I waken up early. Mebbe three or four o'clock, so rather than disturb my wife, I jeest lie there an' think. I imagine I'm back aboard the *Storm Drift*, lyin' shelterin' in a wee corner in Carnan. The win' eases a bit so I mebbe lift the anchor an' set off doon the shore frae Skiport, richt doon by Boisdale, an' intae a' the favourite wee holes we used tae get herrin' in. It passes the time fine, an' if we all come back again an' get anither chance at this auld world, I'll mebbe mind a' they hauls, an' it'll gi'e me a head start on a'body else!'

I spoke recently to one of the older fishermen in Maidens, who told me that he now rarely saw any of his erstwhile workmates except at funerals. Just recently, attending the third funeral of fishermen in as many weeks, he stopped outside the church and spoke to Grieve.

'Aye Matt,' said Grieve, 'the wey things are, it's hardly worth gaun hame. We micht as weel bide in the Kirk till oor turn comes, it'll no' be lang noo!'

Grieve is another definite Captain.

Going south from Dunure and deliberately bypassing Maidens, we come to Girvan, the largest of the fishing towns on the Clyde, which of course also had its share of Captains.

'Jimmy the May', as mentioned earlier, was one such worthy. He seemed totally unafraid of any kind of weather, and the tale was often related to youngsters of the night when he and his ringer, the *AJJ & T*, were caught in the strong tideway off the Mull of Kintyre in a very bad gale. The lighthouse keepers watched him for several hours as he tried to make headway, until the wind eased a bit and he was able to continue his passage to Girvan. When he got in, there was a considerable amount of damage done to the boat and, as soon as they had secured the ropes, the terrified crew resigned en masse. This led to Jimmy saying on many occasions, 'I don't pey them aff, I wash them aff!'

He was at sea at the Manx fishing one wild night when no other pair had ventured out, and had shot his net, resulting in it being brought back aboard with no herring, but suffering quite a lot of damage from the excessive strains caused by the weather. He managed to get his neighbour's crew back aboard their own boat with some degree of difficulty, and their skipper then called to him, 'D'ye ken if there's an asylum on the Isle o' Man?'

'Aye,' says Jimmy, 'I expect there is. Whit wey are ye askin'?'

'Because that's where we should be put for bein' oot here on a nicht like this!'

Alec McCrindle, better known as 'Rin Tin Tin', was skipper of the *Silver Crest* from Girvan, and he was another who could have a book written about him.

I remember him having a machinery failure whilst fishing at Whitby, which meant that he had to have a new crankshaft delivered to him there. This heavy piece of machinery was encased in a wooden crate which was about six feet long, and when it was being lowered on to the deck of his boat on arrival, the activity caught the attention of many of the holidaymakers who idly thronged the piers. The act of getting this expensive load safely on to the deck was accompanied by much shouting and waving of arms.

When it had been safely lowered, Rin Tin Tin looked up at the onlookers, doffed his hat and solemnly but loudly announced 'Dust to dust, ashes to ashes, and thank you all for your kind attendance here today!'

In the years immediately following the war, many manufactured items were perhaps not as good as they might be, leading to the words 'pre-war' being applied to something which had been manufactured in times before hostilities commenced, and which therefore was expected to be of better quality.

The *Silver Crest* had been on the beach at Girvan having her bottom painted, but when it came time for her to be refloated and to resume her fishing effort, all were horrified to find that she would not float because the tides were weakening, and that she was in grave danger of being 'neaped' – that is, stuck there until the tides started to increase again in perhaps two weeks time.

Immediately 'Tarry' McCrindle – another great character – was called upon to assist, as his boat the *Aliped* had the most powerful engine then available. Tarry sprang into action at once, secured a tow rope to the *Silver Crest* and applied the power. The rope snapped! Rin Tin jumped down into the engine room of his stranded boat and emerged soon after with the end of a very heavy rope, announcing, 'This'll dae it.' It was obvious to all the onlookers that this rope had not seen the light of day for many years and, judging by the clouds of dust which arose from it, was well past its 'sell by' date, so no one shared his confidence. However, the tow was passed, the towing boat went ahead, but had hardly taken the strain when the rope snapped.

'I canna' understan' that. It's pre-war, I can assure ye!' was the roar from Rin Tin, a comment which passed into the vocabulary of all the Clyde fishermen, and which is still used when an accident happens through using inferior gear!

7

For our last call in the Clyde we go to Maidens, the place where the idea for this book was conceived. Maidens is a small village between Dunure and Girvan. The little sandy harbour which once housed what was, in my opinion, the finest and the best kept fleet of fishing boats in the world, is now utterly devoid of any sea-going activity of any consequence. The superb fleet which once graced this tiny tidal haven is scattered and gone. It was home in my young days to some of the finest fishermen anywhere in Britain, and they and their boats were admired everywhere they went. Some of these fishermen are still alive today, and it is to the remaining one of a pair of brothers, who epitomised all that Maidens meant in fishing circles, that we turn first.

Matt Sloan lives with his wife in a bungalow in the centre of the village. He still carries himself tall and erect, and displays the powerful physique which enabled him to haul the sole rope of a ring-net faster than the winch which he was supposed to assist!

Indeed, I remember one occasion when they had engine trouble in Mallaig and had herring to discharge. The lack of engine power meant, of course, that the winch was not available for the landing operation, so Matt was hauling single-handed the full baskets of herring from the hold up to the pier – a lift of perhaps thirty feet, and a gross weight of around seven stones. When he was called away to the engineer's workshop in the village, the *two* men who took over this task from him were very soon struggling, and great was their relief when another boat came alongside and they were able to use her winch!

His brother was Billy, now dead. Billy was somewhat different in build, tall and not so heavy, with a slight stoop. He had an almost schoolmasterish air about him. The two brothers served as officers in the Royal Navy during the war, and on the cessation of hostilities, returned to the fishing to make up a team which was pre-eminent on the West coast from the 1950s to the 1970s. In my opinion their strength lay in their differences; Billy was the Cavalier and Matt the Roundhead, to borrow a historical allusion. Billy the laughing brilliant blade, with a razor sharp intellect, and Matt – though equally clever – the dogged plodder who would never know when he was beaten.

They were born into an already-legendary fishing family, all of whom were referred to by any younger fishermen with the prefix 'Uncle', probably as a mark of respect. These famous 'Uncles' – Jake, Jimmy, Billy, and their father Tommy – were unsurpassed masters of their profession, and would have commanded instant respect in any company anywhere in the world.

It was customary at the weekends to haul the ring-nets forward from their usual place of readiness aft, to the forward side deck of the boats, where they were spread out to dry. On more than one occasion one or other of these men requested me to lay out 'hand-holes' for them. These were small holes in the nets which were not of any consequence, and which were usually ignored. They wanted them left out so that they had something to do to while away the time, and sat contentedly mending on a Saturday afternoon and evening. Never on a Sunday though!

Their boats, the *Veronica*, the *Virginia*, the *Wistaria* and the *Watchful*, were immaculate. It was a fact that they were as clean after discharging a shot of herring – a dirty job which scattered scales everywhere – as other boats were when lying idle!

Like all successful men they were single-minded, and their pursuit of the herring took priority over almost all else. They were God-fearing men, however, and would not tolerate any work being done on the Sabbath. There was a ban on all weekend fishing, self-imposed by the fishermen, which was rigidly enforced everywhere except Whitby. There the governing body was composed of Whitby skippers, and they allowed Sunday fishing, as the season there was a very short one. The Sloans, however, and indeed I think the same applied to all of the Maidens fishermen, would not take advantage of this extension to their week, and invariably lay in the harbour until the Sabbath had passed.

One advantage of the care lavished on their boats and gear, was that they were able to work in weather which sent lesser breeds scurrying for shelter in their less well maintained boats. I remember talking to Uncle Jimmy one day as they were discharging a shot of herring, caught when they were the only boats at sea, and he said to me 'Aye boy, I'd raither ha'e fifty cran when there's naebuddy else oot, than the fill o' the boat when a'body has the same!'

Many hours were spent trying to figure out the 'luck' of the Sloans but, in my opinion, if the men so engaged had spent more time at sea, and less in fruitless speculation, they would have been nearer to equalling their successes. I spoke recently to Andy Alexander, who sailed with them for some years, and we touched briefly on the subject of this luck.

He told me of one occasion when they were, as he aptly put it, ploughing Loch Striven in the upper reaches of the Clyde estuary. A small fleet of boats had steamed up to the head of the loch and back down again, without any of them seeing any herring at all. The Sloan brothers continued this relentless, monotonous combing of the loch, from one side to the other, disregarding the rest of the fleet who, having convinced themselves that the loch was barren, had already left. A tiny mark was spotted on the echo sounder. Matt shot, and the result was 800 baskets of prime herring. Luck? Not in my opinion. Sheer dogged persistence is nearer the truth.

On another occasion, a fleet of boats were working in Loch Scridain in Mull. They sought the small herring for which the loch was renowned, but were finding only sprats which made a similar trace on the fish-finding devices. This effort had been going on for some time when the Sloans arrived late in the afternoon, shot, and filled their boats with the only herring to be taken that day!

Again in one of the Mull lochs, Andy told me that one day Matt had been frantically trying to correct a fault in the echo sounder without success. Andy, standing forrad, reported that he could see a seal playing with a herring, throwing it in the air then retrieving it. As the boat passed through this area the sounder started to work of its own accord, marking a large concentration of herring, and continued to function only for as long as it took to shoot the net. It then gave up the ghost and did not work again until professional help had been obtained. It had, however, worked long enough for them to fill the two boats with herring! These were the kind of happenings which fostered the Sloan legend, and they are not isolated events by any means.

In Cockenzie a few years ago, I went into a small fishmonger's shop to ask where I might find a man I wanted to question about fishing activities on the Forth. The man I was asking was around seventy-five years old, very spry and alert for his age, and after he had answered my question, he wanted to know why I was seeking this gentleman. My reply, that I wanted to question him about the ring-net, provoked the following:

'*He* was never at the ring-net! *I* was at the ring-net. In 1935 we went through the Forth and Clyde Canal, tae show thae Wast-coasters hoo tae catch herrin'.

'We went intae Loch Riddon an' felt a guid spot on the wire, so we turned roon an' shot. There was a Clyde man shot alongside us – awfu' namely fur catchin' herrin' he was – I think it was a man ca'ad Sloan, aye, the *Veronica* was the name o' the boat. Weel, we got six baskets, this man got six hunder baskets!

'Show thae men hoo tae catch herrin?

'Na, na! That wan nicht was enough fur me. We were in Greenock the followin' mornin', an' I got the train hame an' got a job on the buses in Edinburgh. War broke oot a year or twa later, an I was in a reserved occupation. Jeest close the door on yer wey oot!'

Billy had a son and a daughter; Matt had five daughters. Matt came ashore from the fishing, to the surprise of many, and started to work in a fishsalesman's office, leaving Billy and his son to fish the two boats. It is my belief that Matt saw the future of the herring industry, didn't like what he saw, and so chose to leave.

Billy carried on fishing for herring, then trawling for prawns and white fish, until one day in the Clyde, after he had taken aboard a good haul of coley, a terrible accident happened.

The weather was bad and a lump of water struck his boat, the *Wistaria*. Two crew men were thrown into the water. Billy instantly went astern to get them back aboard, but unknown to him a part of the net had also been washed overboard. This went into the propeller, disabling the boat, and the two men in the water were drowned.

The two, Cameron Ware and Tom Harvey, had been with Billy for many years and his anguish at seeing them die thus must have been dreadful. When later that day the *Wistaria* reached Ayr, Billy went ashore, never to set foot on the boat again. She was sold. His son Barry then contracted a fatal illness, and just a few weeks before his end, Billy himself died, probably of a broken heart.

Thus ended the Sloan legend, but wherever men talk of herring, their names are spoken of in awe, and they would be wondrous guests around Angus's fireside. Captains? Without a doubt!

At last I come to the man who really started all of this meandering tale, Turner McCrindle.

I visited him some years ago while his wife was still alive, and they were living in their little cottage in Maidens. Going toward the house, I had been telling my wife a little about this legendary man, and as we approached I spotted an open launch around eighteen feet long, lying in the garden. I told Ina to take heed of the condition of this boat, as I was sure that Turner would keep it in the same manner as he had kept all of the ringers he had owned. It was winter time, and the engine had obviously been taken out of her to be stored safely, but the boat surpassed all my expectations. It was varnished inside and out and was absolutely immaculate. I have eaten from tables which looked less clean than the bilges of this wee boat.

Turner opened the door to my knock, and when he finally recognised me and shook my hand, it was like being gripped by a bunch of tarry ropes. He was a big man and had a tremendous aura about him. When I think of the *Saffron*, the *Sapphire* or the earlier *Margarita*, I see the boats dimly, but the oilskin clad figure of Turner stands out tall, unbent and unblurred by time.

We were taken in and sat down, then I asked him what he was doing with himself.

'Ye'll hae seen the wee boat in the garden,' said he. 'I gang tae the screenge net (a small otter trawl) wi' her in the summer months, jeest oot here below the hoose. We get a few plaice. This year was guid, we had 645. Last year wisna sae guid, we only had 482, but the year afore that wis grand, we had abune 700.'

I cannot remember the exact numbers as quoted by him, so have invented them, but if Turner said that he had 482, then you may be certain that that was exactly what he had. When I asked him if this was boxes or stones that he was referring to, he told me that he was enumerating the numbers of fish caught! Not boxes. Not stones. Individual fish!

'I keep a list o' all the puir auld folk in the village,' he replied when I asked if he sold the fish to the hotel, 'an' they all get their turn o' a fry.' Knowing Turner, it would not matter what price anyone offered him for his catch, they would not be able to buy it. It was destined for the 'auld folk' of Turner's choice, though probably most of them were younger than him!

He also told me that he wrote a lot of poetry, and opened a cupboard to reveal these compositions, which were typed for him by a young lady in the village. There were many themes there for us to look at, but most of them had a religious bent, as befitted a man of Turner's faith. When I asked after the health of his brothers, he told me that one brother, Alec, better known as 'Sugar', was dead. 'He died,' said Turner, 'because he went tae the sea on the Sabbath. He had moved tae Stranraer, an' had a wee lobster boat. Weel he went oot on the Sabbath day, the boat upset, and that was the end o' Sugar.' When I said that I hadn't heard of this drowning accident, Turner said that Sugar hadn't drowned but had died some six months later, as a result of the accident.

The McCrindles
(l-r): Alex, Turner, JT, Roy and Bill

I spoke to Bert Andrews, skipper of the *Pathfinder*, in Mallaig some time later, and recounted the tales which Turner had related. Bert, another who tragically paid the price of fish with his young life, lived in Maidens and of course knew Turner well, but his reaction was a revelation to me. Sugar, he told me, had died of cancer, and his death was in no way related to his going to sea on the Sabbath.

'Did he tell you who his crew was on his fishing activities?' Bert then asked me. Turner went to sea with his wife as crew on his small boat! They were in their seventies at this time! Bert said that Turner was convinced that the Fishery Protection patrol was out to get him for his 'poaching', and that when he saw the smoke of their ship leaving Ayr, he immediately hauled his trawl, raced the half mile or so into Maidens harbour, and took trawl, doors and warps up into the store on a barrow!

Turner was one of six brothers, and he was indisputably the dominant one. Although he himself did not go into the wheelhouse of any of the boats which they owned, he dictated where they went, and when. Roy, one of the brothers, often told the tale against himself of the occasion in Oban when they had finished discharging herring late one night and were preparing to go to sea again.

'D'ye think it'd be a guid idea tae get fish an' chips for supper, Turner?' he queried. The answer being 'Aye, I'd enjoy that,' Roy called in his usual peremptory manner to a young lad who had been loafing around the pier watching them work. 'Come here, small boy. Ye'll gang up tae the chip shop an' get six fish suppers richt awa. Noo they're two an' sixpence each, so here's fifteen shillin's an' a shillin' tae yersel' fur going fur them.'

Needless to say, small boy and the money were never seen again!

Turner and his wife were always a team. I remember being in Maidens one spring when our engine was being overhauled by Andy Marr, the marine engineer there, and one evening my uncle Crawford was taken to Turner's house for a meal.

The ringers then all carried old lorry and car tyres – called fenders – on their starboard sides to protect them when they came together at sea, which was a necessary part of the ringing operation. When Turner took Crawford into his house, his wife said, 'I see the *Margarita* is lying port side tae the pier Turner, dae ye no' think that's a guid opportunity tae lift in the fenders an' let the air get roon' the wood below them?'

'That's a guid idea,' said Turner, so he and Crawford went back to the pier and did just that.

When my uncle related this tale, he was of the opinion that no wife of his would ever be allowed to tell him what to do with his boat, but I fear that he was missing the point totally. Turner's wife was just as much a part of the team as he was, and was concerned – rightly - that the boat should be properly cared for.

When I thought quietly over the short time spent with this wonderful old couple, it gradually became an obsession with me that this man and his wife would die one day, and that no tangible record of their remarkable way of life would remain. We daily watch so-called celebrities being fawned over by television interviewers. These self-styled celebrities are mostly balloons filled with nothing more substantial than their own egos, and it might well be fair comment to say that the vast bulk of them are at best, 'legends in their own minds'. I fear that society is built upon a ladder system, where those below support the ones above regardless of worth, in the certainty that they themselves will one day succeed to this artificial grandeur. In my opinion this is a self-propagating cancer which will one day destroy its host. Why was there not a film producer somewhere with the vision to capture something of the life which this couple were living?

I have neither the abilities nor the facilities to catalogue the story of such a giant as Turner McCrindle but, as I thought of it, gradually this book was born as a tiny tribute to his life, and to the lives of the others I would dearly love to meet around the fireside with Angus.

I can see him yet, perched forward on the *Saffron*, his big powerful figure dressed in a yellow oilskin and wearing the paddy hat which always adorned his head. The same figure can be seen again in the dim glow of the double stern light at night, as he still stands with the wire in his hand feeling for his beloved herring.

8

In the early summer of 1956, I left Campbeltown and went to Mallaig, a small West Highland fishing village which clings to the rocks at the mouth of Loch Nevis in what was Inverness-shire. The name of this loch is translated popularly but, as far as I am concerned rather puzzlingly, as 'Heavenly Loch'. Archie MacLellan, hotelier and local historian, told me that his mother – who had worked in the Post Office in the days when telegraphy was the norm, and who was therefore an expert on Morse – told him that when sending 'Inverness-shire' in Morse code as she did many times every day, there were a total of eighteen successive dots to send. Try it for yourself: from the dash in the *n*, to the next dash in the *r* – there are indeed eighteen dots.

It is out of chronological order here, but worth recalling a letter which I wrote to Moira Kerr, who was then editor of the *Oban Times*, as a prank. It went something like this :-

Dear *Rona*,

Islay odds that *Jura* very nice girl, so I thought I'd *Colonsay* that *Iona Barra* and that if you're too *Tiree*d to walk, I'd *Coll* and *Gigha* lift tomorrow. I *Shiant* be late, for *Lewis* and *Ben Becula* are coming too. It is not pie in the *Skye*, and I *Canna Muck* about, nor am I *Uist* to Crow*lin*, but it would be a *Rhum* thing if I couldn't do this without anyone having to *Eigg* me on. It is not *Eriskay* thing to do, but if you think you *Shuna*, I'll understand, but I mu*Staffa*n answer soon.
Yours aye,

Sanday

Moving to the West Highlands is a traumatic event for those who do not understand the people who live there, but I was fortunate in that I had worked among them for some time and had learned something of what made them tick. This understanding – or lack of it – of the people is epitomised by the apocryphal story of the old lady who lived at Ardvaser on the Isle of Skye.

This old dear had developed a very sore throat and had called the doctor in to attend to it. This man had only recently arrived on Skye from the Home Counties, and did not yet understand the innate shyness of the people, making the common yet fatal mistake of confusing this shyness with backwardness. He examined the old lady and wrote out a prescription for a product which he thought would cure the sore throat. Noting as he did this, that the low seat upon which she sat revealed that she wore long red underwear with elastic around the knees, he decided that he could have a little gentle fun at her expense, so he approached her, looked down her throat again, told her to open her mouth really wide and commented 'Yes, I think that the medicine I have prescribed will do the trick. By the way,' – this said peering intently down her throat – 'I notice you are wearing long red bloomers.'

His lesson was learned the hard way when she replied quietly, 'Ah yes, Doctor. Now while you are here, will you have a look up my bum and tell me if my hat is on straight?'

Another story which illustrates the humour of the area concerns the old crofter in Ardvaser who wanted to sell his crofthouse, and who was approached by the ubiquitous rich American who wanted to buy a piece of his forebear's land. He was shown around the house, and expressed delight with all he had seen, but finally remarked of his reservations on the apparent absence of a toilet. The old crofter then took the prospective buyer down through an increasingly muddy field, arriving at a very small, dilapidated wooden outhouse.

'There you are,' he announced, pointing proudly at the bucket inside the hut.

'What about security?' demanded the Yank, looking askance at the huge gaps in the planking of the sides and roof, and at the lockless, ramshackle door which was hanging off one hinge.

'Security?' retorted the old chap. 'My grandfather did his business every day here until he died. My father did his business here until he died too, and I have been doing my business here since I was old enough to walk. Now do you know something, we haven't lost a shit out of it yet!'

The other classic riposte to a smart remark from a Southerner was delivered when two young soldiers, newly posted to the Army rocket range at Benbecula, went into their new 'local' to view the opportunities for some highflying nightlife. The rather limited facilities available in this pub obviously did not meet with their approval, so one of them, having had a good look around, remarked to the other in a loud voice, which was obviously meant to impress the 'natives' who were drinking there, 'I think this must be the arsehole of the world, mate.'

An old chap at the bar put down his whisky, had a pull at his pipe, looked this young soldier up and down and then, fixing him square in the eye, furthered the lad's education by saying quietly to him, 'I wouldn't worry about that if I was you sonny. You're just passing through it!'

Some years ago, a friend and I had, in a misguided moment, become involved in chartering yachts out of Mallaig. During this spell there was an incident which illustrated another facet of the nature of West Highland people, which is often misinterpreted as nosiness.

A group of young people had chartered one of our yachts, and anchored one evening in a bay north of Kyle. They had gone ashore to dine in the local hotel, and met some other yachtsmen there who had invited them aboard their very large blue yacht for a nightcap. Their host, as I remember, was none other than Sir Isaac Woolfson who was, I believe, the owner of Great Universal Stores.

In the morning the youngsters went ashore to the only shop in the village for some food. This shop was self-service, and also doubled as the local Post Office. When they went in, the owner, a burly old chap who smoked a pipe incessantly and who took no active part in the running of the shop, quizzed them relentlessly about their background while revealing none of his own. He was the kind of man who, given an hour with anyone, would be able years later to relate not only their history back as far as their great-grandparents, but would also be able to give a fairly accurate estimate of their bank balance! Sir Isaac then appeared with his wife, so the old chap zeroed in on him, but was instantly struggling because, apart from telling that, yes, the blue yacht which was anchored in the bay belonged to him, nothing else was going to be revealed.

'What line of business are you in then?' asked the old chap.

'Oh, the same as yourself,' was the reply.

'By jove, you must have a big Post Office in your shop to be able to afford a yacht like that,' was the best response the poor old chap could muster.

When I first went to Mallaig as a fisherman, I lodged with David and Rosie McMinn. Rosie is my wife's sister, and I would find it difficult to repay their kindliness to me then.

One weekend, shortly after my arrival there, David developed a severe pain in his abdomen and the doctor was sent for. This doctor was an extremely clever man whose diagnostic skills were legendary among his peers – (indeed, a doctor in Weymouth just ten years ago told me that we were lucky to have had such a skilled man in our community) – but he had a weakness for whisky. When he arrived in the house, it was obvious to me that he had been indulging in this weakness, but he examined David and confidently announced that he was suffering from appendicitis, and that this would of course mean a trip to hospital for its removal. The diagnosis made, he appeared happy to sit down and drink the tea which Rosie had made for him at his request, taking no action to get an ambulance for David, who was now audibly suffering! Eventually the process was started; the local ambulance was summoned and arrived, and off we went on the fifty or so miles of single-track, bumpy road which had then to be suffered before reaching hospital.

Cars were a rarity in those days, so I did not know many of the villages en route to Fort William and hospital, but I now know that we were just a few miles beyond Arisaig when the all of the lights in the ambulance went out, the engine stopped, and the driver shouted, 'Get out, the engine's on fire!'

We did as we were told with some haste, patient and all, but it then became evident that the fire was electrical, and although we were now stranded at the side of the road in total darkness, we were safe! The driver asked me to carry on up the road for about half a mile, where I would find some cottages. I was to knock at the door of one of them, and ask for a loan of a torch – an item which did not appear to be considered a necessary piece of equipment in an ambulance – but which was now essential if repairs were to be made.

I followed his instructions, and found myself running and stumbling along this dark and deserted road, with not a light in sight, at around eleven p.m. on a bitterly cold winter night, wondering why I had ever left home and civilisation! At last I spotted a dim glimmer of light just off the road and, correctly assuming that this was one of the cottages for which I was searching, carefully picked my way down the path to the door and knocked.

Eventually, after much bumping and banging from inside, the door opened, and I excitedly demanded the loan of a torch from the elderly man who now stood in the doorway. I soon realised that the reason for my initial lack of success in my demands, was due to the fact that I was talking much too fast for this poor man who was later described to me as being a refugee from Belgium, for whom English was decidedly a second language! Eventually, however, I arrived back at the disabled ambulance, and Jackie, the driver, commenced repairs under instruction from David the suffering patient, who was fortunately an electrician. The outcome was a happy one, the operation was successfully carried out, but it was literally a baptism of fire for me, and was not the sort of introduction to the emergency services which inspired confidence!

Mallaig is a community of around one thousand souls, which owes its origins to the fact that the small bay which now houses it, was chosen as the railhead and steamer connecting port for the West Highland line. It owes its name to the Vikings – translated it means 'rocky bay'. It has thankfully thus far successfully resisted the efforts of a misguided few to add 'Port of ' as a prefix to this name.

The coming of the railway and the building of a pier opened up the markets in the south, and it rapidly grew in size to service the herring boats which used it. In the early days of Mallaig's growth as a fishing port, the lack of mechanical devices for splitting herring prior to the salting and smoking processes, (necessary to turn them into the kippers for which the port was rightly famed), meant that girls were imported for the task. These hard-working ladies, mainly from the East Coast of Scotland, were housed in huts built adjacent to the kippering plants. Planning controls were conspicuous by their absence, so the huts were built higgledy-piggledy, with little thought for their aesthetic values.

The area which housed the kipper yards and the huts was unimaginatively known as The Point – simply because it was built upon an area which jutted out into the sea, near the pier. I had heard many cautionary tales of the Point at Mallaig, long before I left school, so had looked forward, with some trepidation, to seeing this Soho of the North at first hand when first I came ashore there as a boy. My initially cautious exploration of this place revealed only the scrupulously clean wooden homes of hard-working fisherlasses, whose moral values were generally far higher than those of the fools who had sought to mislead me!

My move to Mallaig was primarily to be near to Ina, the girl who was to become my wife, and who lived there. Her maiden name was Sutherland, and her father, 'Big Willie', had been a notable fisherman with the Mallaig fleet as owner and skipper of the *Jessie Alice*. He unfortunately had died before I came to Mallaig, so my great loss was that I never got to know him personally. Ina's mother was from the famous Mallaig fishing family, the Mansons, and it was with them that I was now about to start work. Her uncle, Jim Manson – Black Jim as he was popularly known – is the first of my Captains there.

He was a big powerful man with a dark, almost swarthy, complexion, and very piercing black eyes. His hair had been black, but was by then almost white. At that time the Manson family owned or controlled four boats, and Jim was very much in charge of every move they made. He dictated when they went to sea, where they fished, and when they came back again. He was, like all successful men, the subject of much controversy, and even now, years after his death, the very mention of his name can provoke much discussion.

There was, despite all his bluster and bravado, a great deal about him which suggested a deep-felt shyness. For example, on the rare occasions when he went on a shopping expedition with his family to, let's say Inverness, he did not want to eat in a restaurant, preferring to have a sandwich or the like sitting in the security of his own car. His model of justice was a mixture of the Judaic ideal of 'an eye for an eye', with a liberal dose of his own sense of fun. He used to say of anyone who had mortally offended him, 'Shooting's too good for that one, he needs a good kick up the arse!'

Jim Manson

A typical week started, of course, with going to sea. The first boat to leave had to be Jim's, simply because he would not tell anyone else just where he proposed that they would fish that night – so no one else knew where to go! This promoted the theory that, because of the typically bad visibility of the driving rain which is so prevalent in the winter, he was never *quite* sure which part of the east coast of the Outer Hebrides he would arrive at; so, wherever they made the shore, that was, they reckoned, the place he would later say he had been aiming for! This slur upon his navigational abilities was stimulated by some of the theories which he expounded at times. For example, he said that, 'If ye're no' sure what side o' a buoy tae go on, keep close tae it. The boat that pit it there draws mair watter than you do!' I don't think I would advise anyone to follow that lead, nor his habit of using a match to measure the distance between two points on a chart. 'A match is aboot an hour's steam,' he would say, taking no heed to the differing scales of the charts which might be in use!

Those statements owed more to his sense of fun than to his ignorance of navigation I am sure, and those who would denigrate his abilities choose to ignore the fact that he never failed to find the West End (of Canna) – a much sought after landmark – on the inkiest black, gale-riven of nights en route to market in Mallaig, and this when a barely reliable compass and a battered old alarm clock were the only navigational equipment to which he had access. His preferred fishing grounds were the rock-infested lochs on the east coasts of South Uist, Benbecula, and North Uist, and over the years he took a vast amount of herring from these areas.

Whilst fishing there, an essential part of the gear kept ready for use was a tow rope, because prudent navigation took a poor second place to the pursuit of his prey, and it was an almost nightly occurrence to have to tow a boat off one of the many rocks. The result of this single-minded chasing of the herring was that his boat, the *Margaret Anne*, was rarely a pleasing sight to the eye of those who did not understand that he did not seem to mind knocking lumps off his boat, if it meant that he was catching herring!

Another result of fishing on these grounds was that there was a lot of damage done to the nets, and it was rare indeed to see the *Margaret Anne* without her deck swarming with crews repairing this destruction. It was common for Jim to lift his anchor and set off fishing earlier than normal when he saw a strange boat approaching, and I am sure that this was done because he did not want them to see the battle scarred boat and net, at close quarters.

He was one of the very few men to whom money seemed merely a necessary evil. For example, he rarely appeared to bother about the price obtained for the herring he had caught. Catching them was paramount in his eyes. He also gave away far more than anyone will ever be able to catalogue. I remember one boat from the Clyde, which had not been enjoying the best of luck, losing her ring-net due to it being washed overboard on a stormy passage across the Minch. This seemed to be the final blow to them, but Jim gave a perfectly good net to this unfortunate man. In today's terms, this gift would be worth in the region of £20,000!

He re-engined a small boat whose owner –from one of the islands – had fallen on bad times. Other gifts, of which I am aware, ranged from radio receivers to refrigerators! I remember asking him why he gave away so much, and will never forget him fixing me with his black eyes, and growling, 'The giving hand's the receiving hand.' Some people of course, took advantage of this philosophy of his.

I personally was annoyed on more than one occasion, when he took a fry of fish which we had caught, and were now looking forward to eating, and gave them to what he thought was a deserving case. It was my jaundiced opinion that the recipients of these gifts were simply scroungers who were down at the boats to see what was on offer! During the spring months, there were often line-fishing boats working in the Minches, and Jim took it upon himself to see that they were kept supplied with the herring which they used to bait the hooks. At this time we were usually fishing in daylight on the west coast of Skye, around the Neist Point area. Moonen Bay, to the south of Neist, was the area where we got the good quality herring, but they were thinly scattered, and to get a marketable amount of them meant a lot of hard work, so as a result it was a relief when darkness came, and it was time to call a halt. Jim had different ideas.

In the shelter of Loch Poltiel there were usually thin scatters of immature herring, so we went there to catch bait for the line-fishers. Having caught the few crans which were needed, one of his boats was then despatched to deliver them to the liners who would be working perhaps two hours steaming away. Our sole reward for these efforts would be a few ling, which the grateful crew of the liner would throw aboard us, and which were subsequently given by Jim to the inhabitants of Poltiel!

Jim had a dark intense air about him which lent itself to the tales which were told about him and several strange experiences which he had known. I asked him about one of these stories, and he confirmed it to me in that odd off-hand way of his.

It had happened when his grandfather, old 'Dodie Bainie', had died and the corpse was being taken back to Buckie in a hearse. Jim told me that he had been sitting in the front seat of this hearse on its journey to the East Coast, when a hand appeared from the roof and rested on his shoulder. Now, if this had happened to me then I am afraid that I would have probably died of fright, but when I suggested this to Jim he just laughed about it and told me that there was nothing to be afraid of! That is not how I viewed it at all.

When the Austin 1100 was first unveiled to the public, everyone was greatly impressed with the then revolutionary new suspension which it featured. This was of course in the days when it was unusual for working men to own cars. Jim ordered one of these vehicles from his usual supplier, a dealer in Fraserburgh, but stipulated that it had to be red. Of course, everyone was keen to see this amazing new model at first hand. We were at sea all week in those days, so it was agreed, well in advance of the probable delivery date, that when it was available for collection, Jim would drive through to Fraserburgh with his son Jimmy and daughter-in-law Violet – who belonged to the Broch, as Fraserburgh is known – in his old car, and trade it in for the new one. This trip would start in the early hours of a Saturday morning, as soon as the boats docked.

One day Violet received a 'phone call from her brother-in-law, Victor, a native of Poland who had settled in the Broch and was a kipperer there, telling her that Jim's new car was in now.

'Oh, that's great,' says Violet, 'fit colour is it?'

'A sort o' maroon shade,' replied Victor

Knowing that the *Mary Manson* was in with herring, Violet sped down the pier to find that the boat was just pulling away en route back to the fishing grounds. She shouted to them, 'Tell Jim his car is in, and it is maroon.'

When we met up with the message bearing boat however, the message was wrongly relayed as, 'Your car is in Jim, an' it's broon!'

'Who the Hell ever saw a broon car,' raged Jim. 'He can keep it. I ordered a red car an' I'm no' gaan tae accept anythin' else!'

When we got into Mallaig on the Saturday morning at around four a.m., young Jimmy went home and was getting ready for bed when Violet got up and started to get dressed, reminding him that they were going to get his father's car. She laughed when her husband said that his father was not going to accept a broon car, and explained the mistake to him. Jimmy got dressed and went to inform his Dad of the error, to find that he was now in bed, and had no intention of getting up again, so the instruction was given that young Jimmy and Violet were to go to the Broch themselves. When they arrived, they went straight to the dealer's garage, and rushed around excitedly, looking for this car.

Seeing a man polishing a green Austin 1100, they asked to be shown the maroon one they were there to pick up.

'This is the only 1100 we hiv,' replied the worker, 'an' it's fur a lad in Mallaig.'

Violet's brother was colour blind!

I am not sure that Jim would be at ease in the crowded room around the fireplace with all the other Captains, but that is certainly where he belongs. Jim had a daughter and two sons. The one remaining son, Zander, is still fishing successfully with his purse-seiner, although the herring-catching scene has changed totally now. William John Manson was a half-brother of Jim's, and he was Chairman of the Mallaig and North-West Fishermen's Association for many years. He is still an active fisherman, and he epitomises the single-minded pursuit of fish, which is all that such men knew.

Duncan 'Porter' Gillies, who owned the *Mallaig Mhor* was another great worthy in the same era as Jim Manson, but unlike Jim, who came to Mallaig from Buckie, Porter was of old Mallaig stock. One of the few who could claim to be a native of the village, he would bring a smile to the faces of the rest of the Captains, and would certainly enjoy a glass of Angus's whisky! It was usual for the ringers in those days to have on board kippers from one of the kippering yards which abounded in Mallaig. Knowing this, crofters on some of the islands would come aboard quite often, looking for a fry. Sometimes they brought a few fresh eggs, scones, or a can of fresh milk, which they offered in return for the kippers.

On the island of Canna, one such man often rowed out to the anchored boat, and he was notable for his habit of knocking on the side of the boat – if the crew were not on deck – until invited aboard. Porter had been a frequent host to this man one week when he had been fishing around Canna, and had, he told me, given the man quite a lot of kippers without anything being offered in return. Arriving back at Canna after landing herring in Mallaig one day toward the end of this week, they had hardly got their anchor down when the worthy appeared again, this time carrying a can of milk. After the usual pleasantries had been exchanged, he asked about the kippers, and it was only then that Porter realised that they had sailed without getting any. On being told this, the man quietly got up and left – taking the milk with him! Porter said that he was speechless: a rare event!

If one of his crew did something slightly wrong Porter used to growl 'If it wasn't Friday, and me a good Catholic, I'd chew the balls off you!' This was, of course, in the days when Catholics were expected to eat fish instead of meat on a Friday. Porter was skipper of the *Mallaig Mhor* for many years, and I do not think that he ever did anyone a knowing wrong. If he couldn't do a good turn, he would not do anything.

A much younger man, though unfortunately no longer with us, was Jimmy Maclean, better known as 'Clainey'. He is definitely one of the Captains who sailed from Mallaig. Clainey fathered seven sons, all of whom were fishermen at some time. Indeed all bar one still earn a living the hard way – from the sea. He was a tall very powerful man who commanded instant respect from all who knew him – respect for the absolute integrity that he displayed in every aspect of his life and his work. He was a nephew of 'Black Jim' Manson, and resembled him closely in appearance and in his life style. His physical strength was legendary, and it was said that he was the only man who had ever broken the perfectly sound cork-rope on a ring-net full of herring, such was his eagerness to get them aboard! John 'G' Henderson, himself a successful skipper of many years standing, told me that in his younger days he had neighboured Clainey, and gave me an instance of the kind of man he was.

They had been anchored one night at the north end of Skye. There was a gale of wind blowing, when another boat dragged her anchor and blew down on top of them, scratching the varnish on Clainey's new boat, the *Minnie MacLean*, in the process. This caused him to jump up and down in temper, but off they went to sea. All night they scoured the stormy waters, seeing no sign of any herring. As daylight broke and the wind eased, they were among the Summer Isles at the mouth of Loch Broom, and had gone alongside one another for a discussion of the options available to them. This action usually meant that the night's efforts were over, and that anchor and sleep were imminent. As they lay there close to the shore, the herring – which had obviously been lying extremely close inshore – did what they often did, rose and played off the shore. John said in describing it, 'The whole sea rose just inside us.' One ring filled the two boats!

The last Mallaig fisherman to be singled out by me as deserving of Captaincy is Willie MacDonald, a native of Benbecula. He was a great church man, was married but with no children, and his favourite pastime on a Saturday night was to wander round to the village shop, where he bought sweets which were then dispensed to the children who gathered around him. Nowadays such largesse would attract the attention of the police, but Willie simply loved children.

He was a very powerful man, with hands like the proverbial shovels! He was a lobster fisherman, skipper of the *Winner*, and in this boat, which was no more than forty feet long, he used to fish as far away as the west coast of the Hebrides on occasion. When fishing there, his wife, who belonged to Cairnbulg on the East Coast, used to say 'Wullie's awa' tae th' Atlantic!'

There are a great many 'nomadic' fishermen who still work out of Mallaig, and from this rich field I would choose one whose presence is essential at Angus's fireside, and who certainly attains the rank of Captain.

George Alexander, known better as 'Dodie Icey' to all privileged to make his acquaintance, hails from Gamrie – or Gardenstown as it is known to some. He was a short round barrel of a man, although the last time I met him and asked how he was, he told me that he had lost some weight, 'half a hunnerwecht' to use his words! Unmarried, he was a kenspeckle figure everywhere he went, dressed in a grey jersey under his neat grey tweed jacket, with a matching 'fore and aft' hat, dispensing pinches of snuff to all those unwary enough to accept this proffered gift.

His accent is pure Buchan, as was used, although not by him, on the famous occasion when two old fellows met one morning when out for a stroll.

'Did ee hear 'at al' Peter wiz deed?,' asked one.

'Na! Fan did 'e dee 'n fit 'id 'e dee o'?'

What would someone from the Home Counties make of that?

He skippered drifters all around Britain, but his last boat, the *Bracoden*, was a steel trawler which he had built for him on the Clyde. I well remember, during one sprat-fishing season, going to him early in the morning on Mallaig pier in order to find out how successful the previous night's fishing had been. In telling of the amounts he thought had been caught, he said, 'Aye, yon local boatie, ye ken, the *Bunch o' Wifies*. Weel he hid twa or three lifts early on in the nicht, but I dinna ken if he got any mair or no'.' I knew full well that there would be sense in what he had just said, but also knew that there was no such craft as the *Bunch o' Wifies*. It was a while before I realised that he was referring to Michael Currie's boat, the *Five Sisters*!

Dodie's observations were legend wherever he went. For example, when he retired a few years ago, he amazed everyone by immediately booking on an extended cruise in a liner. Knowing that Dodie had never done anything like this, and no doubt seeking to air his own knowledge on the subject, a contemporary told him that at some time on this voyage he would be invited to dine at the Captain's table. Dodie's retort – 'Na, na, ah'm no' peyin' a' they bawbees tae eat wi' the crew' – passed instantly into the abundance of tales about the man. He was a very successful fisherman who helped many a young lad get started as a boat-owner and is, as I later discovered, as honest as the day is long.

Gardenstown, his home town, is renowned for the church-going strengths of its population, and Dodie took delight in poking gentle fun at his fellow townsmen on occasion. He once told a spellbound group, who knew that he dabbled quite a lot on the stockmarket, that he had suffered greatly the previous weekend. He had, he said, become convinced on the Saturday morning that he had to sell all his shares in Imperial Tobacco, Distillers, and Scottish & Newcastle Brewers, but had been unable to contact his stockbroker until Monday morning. Asked if he thought that they were headed for a fall, he replied deadpan, 'No, but I jeest took the thocht that if I was tae dee, and a' my neighbours found oot that I had shares in booze an' baccy, they widna' come tae the funeral!'

Dodie is a born storyteller, and for a time I had a good-natured competition going with him, to see who could tell the best story. Each time he landed we each had a story to tell, but I always came off second best. This 'competition' carried on, however, until one day he told one which beat me hollow, and which I have never heard bettered. It was told in his broadest Buchan accent, one which I cannot hope to capture on paper, but which went as follows.

One Saturday night an old bachelor who lived alone in his big family house, decided to have a good look up in the loft. There he found an old fiddle, covered in dust and cobwebs. He took it downstairs, and when he had cleaned it off or, as Dodie put it, 'dichtit it', was amazed to see that it was a Stradivarius.

First thing on the Monday morning he took this priceless instrument, wrapped in a plastic bag, to the local antique shop and announced 'I've got a fiddle for sale here, and it's worth a lot of money.'

'What makes you think that?' replied the dealer.

'Because it was built by Stradivarius,' says our man.

The dealer turned round and shouted through to the back shop, 'What do you think of Stradivarius fiddles, Tam?'

'They're lying all over the place, canna get movin' for them,' says Tam, 'they're not worth anything.'

The dealer then got possession of the fiddle for £50, an offer he made only because, he said, 'I've known you for a long time.'

The old chap was not at all happy, but after a few drams he cheered up, and on the next Saturday night he again explored the loft, this time unearthing an ancient painting which on investigation and severe dichtin was seen to bear the signature of Rembrandt!

Wrapped in the plastic bag, he bore this treasure to the antique shop, first thing on Monday morning, thinking that he'd never be poor again.

'This painting is worth a fearful amount of money,' he proclaimed to the eager dealer, 'for it was painted by Rembrandt!'

'What do you think of Rembrandt paintings, Tam?' the dealer shouts once again through to the back shop.

'Lying all over the place, canna pit my feet down for them. Worth nothing at all,' was the short reply.

'You heard that,' says the dealer, 'but as you are an old friend, I'll give you £50

(l): **Albert Watt, skipper of the** *Ceol-na-Mara* : (r) **'Dodie' George Alexander, skipper of the** *Bracoden*

for it.'

The painting changed hands for this pittance, and off went the old chap feeling decidedly unhappy.

That Saturday night he went to the local fairground where he won two coconuts at a dart throwing stall, so on the Monday morning he took them, in a plastic bag, to the antique shop.

The dealer, seeing him coming, was out like a shot holding the door open for the old man.

'Now then my friend, what have you got for me today?'

'Have you ever heard of *The Wooden Horse of Troy*?' began our ancient hero, taking one of the coconuts from the bag. 'You see, this is one of his bollocks – and before you shout through the back to Tam – the horse only had two and [holding up the plastic bag] I've got the other one here!'

I chanced upon him one Friday on Mallaig pier as he was making his way toward his car preparatory to going home for the weekend. As we chatted, another fisherman called in passing, 'Mind an' keep clear o' —— on your wey hame noo. Nae stoppin' for a dram.' I asked Dodie what place this chap had referred to. He told me, then shook his head and advised me to keep clear of it at any cost. In explanation, he told me that he had gone in one day with two of his pals to this remote country inn for 'a wee dram'.

He was intrigued to see, for the first time, one of 'thae wee things lik a Christmas tree, ye ken fit Ah mean – fan the barmaid pits a gless ower them an' presses doon, they firl roon an' roon, an' watter scoots a' roon aboot the gless, an' washes it. Weel, there wis an aul' lad sittin' in the corner eatin' crisps an' drinkin' a pint o' beer. Fan he hid finished, he squeezed past us an' leant ower the bar, an' then he took oot his falsers an pit them ower this thing tae wash all the bits o' crisps awa'!'

Many of Dodie's stories had a wee sting in the tail as instanced in the following:

❀

A fishing skipper decided that it was time that his son had a boat of his own, so to that end they both went to visit the three banks in their home town, to see which offered the best rate of interest. The son was sworn to silence during the times they were doing the negotiating.

Bank number one agreed to loan the money on the father's security, and would charge a rate of twelve percent, but the father's next question, 'Hoo often d'ye hae a bath?' puzzled the son as much as the banker, who answered 'Every morning of course,' in deference to what he obviously thought was an eccentric potential customer.

Bank number two was visited, and offered them the money on exactly the same terms. This time the question, 'Hoo often d'ye hae a bath?' brought the reply that the puzzled banker had a bath and a shower on alternative mornings.

The third banker offered similar terms, and in reply to the same question asked of the previous two said, 'I bathe every evening before retiring, of course.'

When the pair had left the third bank, the son's curiosity at last caused him to break his vow of silence and he asked, 'Fit wey are ye speirin' at they lads hoo often they hae a bath, Da?'

'Weel, ma loon,' the father replied, 'if ye're gan' tae hae tae kiss they lads erses for the next twenty years, it's as weel tae ken hoo clean they are!'

I personally missed Dodie a lot when he retired, and not just for his stories. It is my considered opinion that any young man, whether fisherman or not, could do a lot worse than model himself on this Captain.

While I was still going to sea, there was a small fleet of seine-netters, most of them from Lossiemouth – the Scottish home of this method of catching fish – working around Coll and Tiree. They chatted almost incessantly on their radios. This was a nuisance to those trying to make contact with someone on the same frequency, but it was a source of information on fishing generally, and provided additional entertainment on dull watches crossing the Minch.

I remember hearing one skipper complain that his Decca (an electronic navigational device) had failed. As his radar had also failed the previous day he now asked if 'Anybody kens hoo tae work they compass things?!'

Seine-netting consisted of shooting great lengths of rope to which the net was attached, in a triangular pattern. The ropes were bought in 'coils', each coil being 120 fathoms, or 240 yards long, and the skippers measured distances in coils rather than the more conventional yards or miles.

This fact was brought home quite comically when idly listening to the long-winded story of how one narrator, a seine-net skipper, had spent the previous week-end. We were treated to a minute-by-minute description of how he and his wife had spent all their waking hours on the Saturday, then he moved on to the Sunday. After a nice breakfast, which was carefully itemised, they had gone to the Kirk. A lunch, equally well-documented followed this, then they had gone for a drive around the countryside near their home.

He then told how he had, 'Cam tae yon little wee roadie, ye ken, the first on the left comin' north oot o' Elgin. We hid nivir been up that way, so I canted the car, an' off we goes. Weel, we hid only got aboot five coil up this roadie, when we cam' tae a dead end...!'

He was not trying to be funny; he lived on the sea and for the sea, and distances – be they on land or sea – were measured in coils, not miles. Boysie qualifies as a Captain in anybody's book, not just mine!

One of my favourite watch-mates of this period was Jimmy Coull, a cousin of my wife. Jimmy was a well built chap, a very competent fisherman, who had travelled a lot and whose tales of his experiences lightened many a weary hour on watch. He and one of his pals, had bought a small car – which must have been one of the first in Mallaig – and the ploys which they got up to in this car were legion.

On one occasion, he told me, they had set out to visit Jimmy's brother who was in the Services, and was then stationed at the airfield near Lossiemouth. They had visited several hostelries en route – this was, remember, before the advent of the breathalyser – and were eventually granted access to the airfield itself. Jimmy said that he only realised how much alcohol they had consumed when his pal who was now driving down the runway, commented to him, 'Smashin' roads they've got on the East Coast, eh!'

The pair of them developed a liking to poultry, and my mother-in-law, who at that time kept hens, was losing one or two just about every weekend. Her complaint to the Police was withdrawn when she discovered that it was two of her nephews who were guilty! Jimmy took this liking for poultry with him when he joined the Merchant Navy, and was only cured of it after one unfortunate experience in Stranraer.

One winter, he had been ashore with some of his mates, and had succumbed to temptation when they passed a hen-house on their way back to the ship. They arrived in their mess with the results of the raid, and plucked the unfortunate fowls before cooking and eating them. The feathers were disposed of by putting them into the fire.

They were visited in the morning, before they were awake, by the Police, who asked where they had been on the previous night. This question answered, the next one was an enquiry as to when they had last eaten chicken?

'Chicken?,' was the reply. 'Ye're lucky tae get corned beef on this ship. We haven't seen chicken for years.'

They were then invited to accompany the police on to the deck. Their case was completely destroyed! Snow had fallen after they had come aboard, and the ship was covered from stem to stern with the feathers which had blown, unburnt, up the chimney, and which were now sticking to the snow!

I am certain that Jimmy would contribute much more than his share of stories to the company around the fire in Angus's home.

Sandy Scally was another favourite shipmate of this era, and was one who confounded all of the medical theories about longevity. A thin man of medium height, he ate sparingly, drank unbelievable amounts of strong tea, and smoked Woodbine cigarettes almost incessantly – yet he lived into his eighties. He also had a great love for Guinness.

Sandy's stories about himself were unique in that they almost all ended in personal disaster. He was a very accomplished goalkeeper in his youth whilst still living in his native Campbeltown, and he told us that, after one cup game, played in a blizzard in Glasgow, he was approached by a scout for Third Lanark who promised him a trial, and prophesied that he could have a good future as a professional. This scout – who had been soaked and frozen whilst watching the game – promptly caught influenza and died before taking the matter of poor Sandy's new career any further! It might be worth noting that the team for which Sandy kept goal so well was one of the most accomplished ever produced in Campbeltown, and that it rejoiced in the name 'The Currant Buns'!

He had come to Mallaig initially to work for a kipperer best known by the nickname 'Waldy', who was married to a lady called Mary-Ann whose strength of character more than compensated for her lack of stature. Mary-Ann ran a small shop, and kept a very firm grasp of the purse strings of their combined enterprises. Their one luxury was a car which neither of them could drive, this task being entrusted to Sandy. Waldy was fond of a dram, but usually could only indulge in this passion when, somehow, he was able to skin some cash. One method that he used was to get the salesman to overcharge his poor wife for the shop herring, the difference being given to Waldy in cash!

One Sunday Waldy appeared at Sandy's door in a state of great agitation. Mary-Ann had fallen asleep in front of the fire; Waldy had removed the key of the shop from around her neck without disturbing her, and was now hell-bent on getting drink!

'It was like one of these bank raids you see in films,' said Sandy. 'I stopped outside the shop, keeping the engine running, while Waldy in a panic-stricken rush unlocked the door, dashed in, and grabbed a paper bag containing the Saturday's takings from the counter where his wife had left it ready for paying into the bank on Monday morning. He stuffed it into his coat pocket and, hardly taking time to lock the door, shot into the back of the car and we screamed off.

'We made straight to Lochailort Inn for a dram, went into the bar and Waldy took out the bag of cash. It was a pound's worth of pennies he had grabbed, just enough to buy the petrol we needed to get us back home!'

Like so many of his contemporaries, Sandy was in the Royal Navy during the Second World War, in the engineering branch. He told me that, for part of his initial training as a stoker, he was taken to a field where stood a steel mock-up of the doors to a ship's furnace. In front of each door there was a large pile of small stones. He and his companions were instructed to choose a pile, and then to shovel the stones through the door. When the pile was levelled, they were to go around to the other side and shovel them back again!

Apart from breakfast the two main meals of the day in the Navy were dinner, served around midday, and supper, which took place around six p.m. Between these two meals, 'tea' was served at around four p.m., and usually consisted of bread or cake of some kind. Sandy woefully told me that one day he was given three winkles for his tea. That there was not a pin issued to eat this feast with, was of no consequence – he didn't like them anyway!

He had also been aboard a mine sweeper berthed on the lower reaches of the Seine when hostilities ceased. They were engaged in mopping-up operations there. One day a draw was held aboard to decide which one of the crew was to be the lucky recipient of the free room gifted by the management of a Parisian hotel. The prize consisted of room and food only. Sandy's name was drawn out of the hat, but he was unable to accept this once-in-a-lifetime prize, as he was stony broke and was unable to raise the fare to Paris!

In 1964, I left the fishing, and came ashore to work. This decision was prompted by several reasons, but the main one was that the whole fishing scene was changing, and I did not like much of what I saw. Large powerful trawlers were taking over from the ringers, and I simply did not want to be part of what was now going on.

I became the mechanic on the local Lifeboat, and took up part-time work in the fish market.

Sandy Scally

9

Working on the pier was being at the hub of the entire life of the village, and that meant that I was now in a position to meet, and get to know, men who were involved not only in the catching of fish, but in the marketing of it also.

When a boat came in with a shot of herring, a random sample of around fifty herring was taken ashore in a basket. A ticket was placed in the basket giving the boat's registration number, and an estimate of the amount of herring in crans. The herring were auctioned by the salesmen, and were bought by buyers who wanted the kind of herring that each sample indicated were available.

There were, of course, malpractices on each side. Sometimes a boat would purposely omit small herring from the sample, making the catch look better than in fact it was. If a boat had only a few crans aboard, and it was not economic sense to go to market, they might keep them aboard, hoping to get more herring on the coming night. They were expected to declare these overdays' herring, but as they were generally worth less, the temptation was to mix the overdays with the fresh. The same was done, on occasion, when the boat had two different kinds of herring aboard. A sample of the larger ones was sent up but, when discharging, the small were mixed in with the large. In order to regulate the industry and to resolve disputes, the samples were kept until the boat had finished discharging, and in the event of a dispute this sample was compared, by an independent source, with the herring actually being delivered.

On the buying side, the buyer often made a mistake, and paid more for the herring than they were worth, or – more commonly – discovered after he had bought them that there was a good fishing coming, which meant that the price would probably drop. Then he would chuck or 'cast' the herring, which meant that he stopped the boat discharging, saying that the herring were not up to the sample, and the independent arbiter, mentioned earlier, was called in to sort out the dispute.

There were many tricks employed to ensure that the unscrupulous buyer won the chuck. He might gain access to the sample and remove from it the percentage of smalls, making them seem to be better than they were. The ticket might be swopped with one from a boat which had an honest sample of large herring, and it was not unknown for samples to disappear on occasion!

If the chuck was upheld – and they seemed to be, more often than not - then the herring were offered for re-sale, often being bought by the same buyer for a lesser price. It was said to me on more than one occasion by many different fishermen, 'When the good Lord appointed his disciples there were a lot of fishermen, but there wisny wan buyer amang them!'

A cran used to be a liquid measure, and so the baskets – made of wicker and stamped with a Crown to show that they were an approved size – had to be

'Off the Road' at Kinsadel, near Mallaig

During a fish auction on Mallaig Pier
(l-r): seated – Donny Hector MacLellan; seated in boiler suit – Sandy Reid
rolled up shirt sleeves – Tom Ralston

properly filled. The cry from the buyer was ever, 'Keep them baskets full noo!' Now the measure is one of weight, and a set of scales has replaced the native skill and wit which was required then.

At the Isle of Man fishing, the great bulk of the market on the island was for the kippering trade and, when this demand had been satisfied, the remainder was very often disposed of for fishmeal. This meant that the boats so affected had to steam the five hours or so to Portpatrick; before leaving Peel, they were issued with a 'redirection chit', which entitled them to the princely sum of something like twenty-five pence or so per cran for their trouble. There were at this time two or three quite small local boats, who were still fishing with drift nets and they, because they were probably still hauling at daybreak unlike the ringers, were usually last into their home port of Peel. It was felt that the 'first come first sold' system then in use was unfair to them, so a scheme was evolved whereby when the sample was taken to the sales ring, the skipper of the selling boat put his hand into a box and withdrew a numbered disc. This fixed the selling order. The lowest numbers were always sold first and, of course, were less likely to suffer the time-wasting nuisance of being redirected.

Of course this system was abused; if a low number was drawn, instead of re-turning it to the box when the sale was over as was expected, the unscrupulous ones would palm their low number for use again the following morning. There were continual rows and accusations over this, but it took everyone a wee while to discover that three boats, who were working together, had evolved a different system. If they had enough herring to warrant having some in each boat, then two set off direct to Portpatrick. The third went into Peel, took three deliberately poor samples up, produced the three high numbers which they had acquired, and so obtained the redirection chits for the other two which by now had probably started discharging in Portpatrick. This strategy gained them quite a few precious hours, but I think I remember it resulted in their being fined by their fellow fisherman when they were discovered.

My move ashore was made at a time when herring fishing methods were changing – a change which led to Mallaig becoming, for a time, the premier herring port in Europe, but which also led to the destruction of the fishing in-dustry as I knew it. As pair trawling was perfected, it started gradually to oust the ringers, and the few remaining drift-net fishermen seemed to disappear overnight. Purse-seining, when it got under way, was such an efficient way of killing herring that there was no longer any room for less competent methods.

The drifters were larger and more powerfully engined than the ringers, and were therefore able to be adapted to continue fishing herring using the mid-water trawl – thereby delaying their demise – but the ringers were quickly relegated to fishing for prawns. On the shore side of the industry, changes had to be made rapidly in order to keep pace with the greatly increased volume of fish being landed.

The pier used by fishermen at Mallaig was made of wood, and owned by British Rail. Not enough money was being spent on its upkeep, and it was an almost daily occurrence for a lorry, loaded with herring, to break through the wooden surface of the pier with one of its wheels and as a result, shed part of the load. This was good for the seagull population, but was not acceptable to anyone else. With hindsight it is obvious that a new harbour facility had to be built, and its existence today will be a memorial to the one man, Gordon Jackson, better known as 'GG', who had not only the foresight, but the ability and the courage to take the required action in forming what is now Mallaig Harbour Authority.

He succeeded, under the auspices of this Authority, not only in raising the finance to take over responsibility for the running of the pier as it was, but – despite fierce opposition from some of the locals whose eyes were firmly fixed on the past – was instrumental in having the harbour rebuilt so that the shore facilities could cope with the vast increase in landings. The pier could now support the weight of the biggest lorries which flooded into Mallaig from all over Europe, and the harbour was able to cope with the influx of the large steel purse-seiners. There was an atmosphere of excitement around, which attracted many extrovert characters to the community of buyers on the herring scene, and I do not think that it would be out of place to recall some of these people now.

Sid Grainger immediately springs to mind, epitomising the type of men then around. He was a native of Hull, and was employed as a buyer for one of the biggest herring processing firms in Scotland. The work he was doing meant that he spent most of his time in lodgings, away from the restraining influence of a wife – an influence which is necessary to us all! – and as a result, his marriage suffered badly. He could well be described as the life and soul of the party, and his fun-loving nature helped to lighten what was often a very stressful time. Sid often sang at parties and in pubs, accompanying himself on the guitar, favouring modern songs. One night this led to confrontation with another buyer.

While Sid was singing his usual favourites, he was constantly being interrupted by a colleague, Bruce, from the north-east of Scotland, who was demanding to hear 'The Northern Lights o' old Aberdeen.' Sid suffered these interruptions for a time, then suddenly stopped playing.

'Did I ever tell you about the time I accidentally stood on a leprechaun and killed him, Bruce?'

The reply being in the negative, Sid continued: 'Well, the King of the Leprechauns put a curse on me. Yes, the curse was that every time I started playing, some idiot would interrupt me and ask me to play "The Northern Lights"!' Instant war resulted!

One day in July – normally a quiet month as far as herring fishing went – Sid appeared driving a new car which had been supplied to him by 'the firm'. Two days later he came to me very early in the morning and asked me to take him to his car to collect some of his gear, as he had, he explained, 'A bit of bother with it last night.' I drove him to the bottom of a hill in the middle of the village, and was amazed to see this sparkling example of automotive excellence lying upside down among some rocks beside the road, with broken glass sparkling in the warm, bright July sun. We got out of my car, and while I was still trying to fathom just what had happened, the local police sergeant arrived on the scene.

'What happened here, Sid?' began the sergeant.

'Fog and black ice, Willie,' was the instant response from the intrepid Sid!

Such was the charisma of the man, that Willie just shook his head, and having made sure that no one had been injured in the incident, he went on his way.

Sid was engaged in a very highly competitive and cut throat business, but to my knowledge he never stooped to underhand tactics in order to gain advantage over any of his fellow-buyers, which cannot be said for many of the rest of us.

He once said to me, 'I was invited to a reunion party for kamikaze pilots at the weekend but I left early as there was no one else there.' If we could bend the rules of this book slightly, Sid, his guitar, and his ready quip, would soon charm our Captains round to his way of thinking.

Of the older breed, two men cannot be ignored. Hendry Young and Roddy MacKenzie had both perfected the art of making kippers, the like of which we will never taste again. Of the two, I believe that Hendry had the edge on Roddy in making kippers, but Roddy was without doubt the most skilful buyer I have ever met anywhere. Hendry latterly would not leave the yard while his beloved kippers were being smoked, and slept beside the kilns more often than he slept beside his wife! When eventually he retired, all he got was a gold watch and thanks – a miserly reward in my opinion from a firm to which he had devoted most of his life. Roddy was in semi-retirement when he occasionally deputised for the then regular buyer for MacRae's, and it was on one of these occasions that I witnessed him, with one stroke of sheer brilliance, completely destroy the inflated self-esteem of one of the major buyers of the day.

It happened late one afternoon. A large trawler had come in with 300 crans – a big shot indeed. We had not been told in advance of this landing, the boat's radio having failed, so all the buyers thought that the only outlet for these herring would be through MacFisheries, to be sold at the minimum price for export which was something like £3 a cran. MacRae regularly bought something like ten crans late in the day, to provide their kipper-house with an early start on the following morning, but *they* had to pay the regulation home market price price of £5 10s a cran. The expectation, therefore, was that Roddy would buy his ten crans at this price; MacFisheries would then mop up the balance. (At auction, when the salesman 'knocked down' the herring to the successful bidder, the buyer stated how much he wanted and the remainder was put up for bids again.)

We were not too surprised when the MacFish buyer – 'Woody' – started (apparently in fun) to chase Roddy up to an unbelievable £10 a cran. Roddy took his usual ten crans at this price, looking daggers at Woody, and turned away in disgust. At this, Woody offered the salesman £3 a cran for the remaining fish.

'Na, na,' said Roddy, turning again to the salesman, 'he's not gettin' them for that!' and off they went again, this time to £8, when Roddy took five crans before again making for the door.

'£3 for all that's left?' said Woody.

Back came our hero, who had been half-way out of the door.

'£5 10s,' he shouted angrily, and turning to the salesman said, 'I'm no lettin' him off wi' that. I don't want them all, but he'll pay the same price as I paid. Come on, £5 10s again!'

At this Woody laughed and said to the salesman, 'Gi'e him what he wants.'

Incredibly Roddy said 'I'll take the lot!', leaving Woody visibly shaken by this audacity.

Roddy later told me that he had been told to buy this shot almost at any price, and he knew that Woody had had similar instructions. He had run a fearful risk in taking only five crans at £8, because Woody – as was his right under the auction rules – could easily have grabbed all of the balance at the same price!

Characters also abounded on the railway, which was a powerful force in the area. The railway tracks at this time ran all the way down the pier, and two steam cranes were engaged nearly all the time, lifting loads of herring boxes into wagons, and helping discharge the heavy cargo from the *Loch Seaforth*, when she arrived early in the morning from Stornoway. It was the duty of one of the crane drivers to use it to shunt goods wagons down the pier, to clear the way for passengers embarking from the steamer who were going to the railway station. This done, he was then expected to unshackle his crane from the wagons so that they could be pulled back, into their position of readiness beyond the station buildings, by a steam engine.

One morning, a stalwart by the name of Angus Cameron, better known as 'Angus the Cran Man' (yes, cran – crane does not rhyme with man!), had done his duty and, wagons in tow, had stopped his crane abreast of the *Loch Seaforth*. One of her crew, on seeing Angus's red face deduced, correctly, that he was suffering from a severe hangover, and invited him aboard for the traditional cure. Angus was enjoying the second half of this cure when he heard the whistle of the railway engine as it started to pull the wagons back up the pier, and he suddenly realised that in his hurry to partake of the golden libation, he had neglected to uncouple his crane.

The sight of the diminutive Angus running full tilt up the pier after his crane, screaming Gaelic oaths as he did so, and of his despairing wails as the jib of the towed crane demolished a goodly part of the station roof, will live for ever in the memory of those lucky enough to have witnessed it.

The driver, fireman, and guard of a 'fish special' seeing that – at seven a.m. on New Year's morning – there was still life in the railside house where 'Woody' lived, stopped and went in to wish all a 'Happy New Year!'

Another train was stopped as it left Fort William, on a very warm day, so that the fireman could get an ice cream from a nearby shop for the signalman a mile or so ahead.

I do not think that we shall see such happenings in the squeaky clean days of the super efficient, squealing-wheeled Sprinters. Perhaps it is just as well, but I for one am glad that I lived in these days!

Of course, there were also on the pier at this time men who, although not buyers themselves were, if anything, more indispensable than anyone in the day to day running of the shore side of the operations.

One of them, Donnie 'Hector' MacLellan, was a driver with British Rail, but every spare moment he had was spent in working – and working very hard – on the pier. We often used to speculate just when Donnie got any sleep. He was of average height, was of a very wiry build, stuttered slightly, except when he sang, and was a fanatical Celtic supporter. I think he celebrated for months after they had won the European Cup.

Perhaps his worst moment occurred one day when he had fallen heir to a couple of boxes of haddock. Donnie managed to get them, unseen, onto the engine, which he then had to drive to Fort William, and spent a good part of the journey filleting them. His mistake was to dump all the offal at the side of the track in the fish boxes which had contained the haddock. The offal was, of course, discovered by the track maintenance squad, and the resulting inquiry as to the origins of these fishy remains concluded with poor Donnie being given two weeks suspension!

He once asked me for, and was given, a boil of expensive prawns. He said that they were to be a present for 'A priest who is on holiday before going to a foreign mission in Africa, and who is staying with my mother.' Weeks later, I discovered that they were in fact given to the owner of a local public house in return for a dram!

Probably as a result of his slight stutter, he tended to talk in a form of shorthand, never using two words where one would do. One night the diesel engine which he was driving broke down just short of Morar. Donnie went to summon help from, well, where else but the bar of the Morar Hotel?

'What brings you here at this time of night?' asked the barman, after he had served Donnie with a dram.

'Power eh eh nowt,' was the short reply!

Donnie, with his bosom pal Charlie MacPherson, were just about the hardest workers anyone could hope to meet anywhere. Charlie had been dux of Broadford School, and would have gone far were it not for his love of whisky, which he shared with Donnie, and whom he resembled closely in build. The pair of them used to spend any leisure time they had on the pier repairing wooden fish boxes, and always had a stock of liquid refreshments (funds being available!) hidden close at hand in case a sudden attack of thirst came over them. One Christmas we were all amazed to see, printed in the *Oban Times* among the usual 'Seasonal Greetings to Customers', one apparently from 'Donnie and Charlie, proprietors of the Pier Bar,' wishing all their 'customers' a Happy Christmas. We never found out who had put the ad in the paper, but Donnie and Charlie took it well.

It was not unusual for this pair to spend all night working aboard one of the klondykers, helping to load and ice the herring bought for export, and then come ashore in the morning to help load some of the lorries which carted the fresh catches off to the Continent. This was very heavy work, and they must have longed at times for a gale to put paid to the fishing effort, and give them some rest. I am sure that Charlie will forgive me if I tell one more story about him.

Shortly before the ban was placed on herring landings, I had a contract to salt ungutted herring into barrels for a Dutch customer. This work was labour intensive and also required the use of a fork-lift truck.

Charlie at this time was driving one for a local fishsalesman, and he offered not only to supply 'his' truck, but also undertook to ensure that the labour demands, which varied from day to day, were met as required. These offers I gratefully accepted, and Charlie was hired! There were a few mackerel, which had to be kept out of the barrels, mixed among the herring, and which were, I thought, being dumped. Some months later, long after this salting episode was over, Charlie furtively asked if he could talk to me privately.

He had, he told me, a potentially lucrative contract to supply a lobster fisherman on Mull with bait for his creels, but lacked the cash to transport it to the customer. If I would pay the transport costs, I could have half of the profit. This sounded like a good deal to me, but I later discovered that the bait was in fact the mackerel, which I thought had been dumped and which had already been paid for by me. They had been salted in my salt, and the containers were the barrels belonging to the Dutchman! Charlie's sole contributions were his labour, his foresight, and his native wit – a formidable combination indeed.

I can see Donnie and Charlie sitting quietly by Angus's fire, glass in hand, listening to the yarns!

Native wit was exemplified by a story told to me by the late Charles Simpson, an oil merchant in Mallaig. The incident had taken place some years before when coal was king, and Charles had a lorry which was kept in a garage attached to a local hotel, and which was used to make deliveries of coal.

One morning, Charles went to get the lorry out for the day's deliveries, and noticed a freshly killed hind hanging up to mature in the hotel garage. His companion who must remain nameless, for reasons which will become obvious, commented on this hind and made much of the delights of a feed of venison.

The following day, the local bobby sought out Charles and his companion, and ascertained from them that yes, they had seen this beast, and that when they last saw it, it still had four legs! Someone, the bobby told them, had stolen a haunch from this hind, which belonged to the proprietor of the hotel, but if it was returned, no more questions would be asked.

It was by now obvious that Charles's companion was guilty, but despite repeated requests he refused to admit to the crime, nor of course would he return the haunch. The bobby asked him for a look at his knife, and when it was guilelessly handed over, he announced that this knife would immediately be sent for police laboratory tests, which would show if it had been used to cut the venison, and that our [clearly guilty] man had one more chance to repent.

This last chance spurned, the bobby strode off, raging that the knife would now definitely be sent for test, and that a jail sentence was likely as a result.

When he had gone, Charles said, 'Did you take the venison?'

'Oh, yes,' was the reply.

'Then you'd better go after the bobby and tell him, because the test will show up traces of blood, no matter how well you have washed it,' said Charles.

'No it won't,' said the guilty party. '*This* is the knife I used to cut it.'

Yes, he had two knives in his pocket, and had handed over the 'innocent' one!

This same man was a native Gaelic speaker, and was never entirely at ease when perforce he had to use English. He obviously thought in his native tongue, and when he was under any kind of pressure, he made mistakes in translating his thoughts into the alien language. On being served with a plate of very thin soup one day on a boat where he was a crew man, he cried, 'Two peas and a barley, and you call that a soup!' Questioned one day by a holiday-maker as to how long the fishing boats remained at sea, he replied, 'Ah well, some weeks they stay out for a fortnight!' His most notable error, as far as I am aware, was when he made the heartfelt cry one day: 'If you came through what came through me, you'd know all about it,' but this mistake must be closely pursued by another made whilst attempting to forecast the weather, when he said 'The sky's away to the north, there'll be more weather tomorrow!'

There are a great many tales which might be told of some of the characters in and around Mallaig concerning the local pastime of poaching. This was not the kind of work which is popularly described now as being carried out by gangs of criminals in high powered vehicles, but was claimed, with a degree of justification, as being the right of the locals to take 'one for the pot'.

Indeed I have often wondered how a Sheriff would deal with the claim, from an accused poacher, that they would instantly return to the sea any salmon which bore a label declaring that it was the property of the Laird!

During one such poaching escapade, which was led by a man who was renowned for his coolness, a stag was shot whilst they were high up on a ridge on one of the islands. As he and his companion approached, this poor beast was seen to stagger to its knees. They ran up to it, to discover that it had been stunned by the bullet, so the companion of our hero prepared to finish it off.

'No, don't shoot him just now,' says our man calmly, 'we'll walk him down to where the boat is, then you can shoot him. That'll save a lot of carrying!'

The same man came home one day, to discover that the local police sergeant had visited his home (on hearing that another poaching expedition had just taken place) and had been allowed access by his wife. The sergeant had taken away a haunch of venison which would, he told the wife, be the evidence against her husband. He had also confiscated a (properly licensed) rifle. This information necessitated a prolonged visit to the local hostelry, where the 'poacher' received a lot of sympathy, and whisky, to help the thought process!

Returning home later that night, he noticed the sergeant's car parked at the rear of the police station. Investigation revealed that the 'evidence' was still in the unlocked boot of the car, so he quietly liberated it, throwing the venison as far as he could into the sea. The following morning he went to the police station, and quietly asked for his rifle back. This politely phrased request was granted in a less than friendly manner by the hopelessly outwitted sergeant!

There was another episode where a poacher – not the same man – displayed a remarkable degree of calmness in adversity. With two companions, he had made the long trip by boat to the head of a sea loch near Mallaig to try for a few salmon. When they arrived, and had carried the net up the shore toward the first of the pools where their prey might be lying, they were horrified to spot three men approaching from landward, obviously with the same objective in mind. They had come to the spot by land, which had involved them in several miles of hard walking. You would be excused for thinking that a 'Mexican stand-off' might be the result of this confrontation, but our subject was made of sterner stuff than that!

Telling his two companions to lie low, our friend donned his 'fore and aft' hat, (an adornment which was favoured by all ghillies), adopted a very pugnacious attitude and a cultured accent, and told the competition in no uncertain terms to 'Clear off my land immediately!' As soon as the hapless trio had hurriedly complied with this demand, and he had succeeded in stopping his friends' laughter, our intrepid lads set about the work in hand.

Another episode, which had a rather less happy ending as far as the poaching fraternity was concerned, occurred when a pair of heroes set out to 'do' a river, some distance from Mallaig. They made their way there via half of the Public Houses in Lochaber, and as a result, on the final leg through the heather toward the targeted pool, they felt obliged to rest for a while among the bracken which lined the river's edge, and promptly fell asleep.

Their snooze was disturbed when a man fell over their recumbent bodies in the half light of the summer's night, and when he had recovered from the shock, he demanded to know who the pair were, and what they were doing. They, in turn, thinking that this man was on the same mission as themselves, and being fully conversant with the ploy used by the gentleman in the last story, told him in perfect Anglo-Saxon to 'go forth and multiply', at the same time questioning him as to just who he thought he was anyway!

When this angler (for such he was) told them that he was a Chief Inspector in the Strathclyde Police, the only reply in their books for such atrocious lies was for one of them to take a swing at him, for daring to think that they were stupid enough to believe such a tall story. Unfortunately for them, his description of his profession was absolutely correct; his only omission being in not telling them that his two, hitherto unseen, companions were also policemen! Fortunately for our two poachers, when they had been duly summoned to appear and explain their actions to the relevant body, the court seemed to see the funny side of the charge. I am sure that Charlie, who is the one surviving victim of this misunderstanding with the police, would agree that they got off lightly in the end.

When the great boom in herring landings from the Minches took place in the early seventies, one man did much more than most to ensure that the many and diverse needs of the fleet were met, and he must therefore instantly qualify as a Captain.

James Hepburn was, and still is, a short rotund man with a beaming round red face below a shining bald head. Everyone, regardless of their station in life, was greeted with a ready smile and the call, 'How's it going, me old fruit?'

He was manager of the main fishsalesman's office. This task was a very demanding one; not for him a 'nine to five' work load. Landing of herring continued for as long as it took to finish the job, so James was in demand for twenty-four hours a day, seven days per week. Herring sales started at eight a.m. on a Monday morning, and continued for as long as necessary until eight p.m. each day; on Saturday the last sale was at midday. No sales were permitted on Sundays. He not only had to cope with trying to satisfy the many demands of fishermen, but had to make the difficult decisions of who among the many buyers were in a sound financial state, and were therefore credit-worthy.

The pressure on him must have been immense, so on more than one occasion he took off with his beloved accordion and found relief in a ceilidh somewhere. His brother told me that, one Sunday, he and his wife had gone for a drive down toward the Ardnamurchan peninsula, and en route they had pulled into a hotel seeking lunch. There, in the middle of an otherwise empty car park, lay James's accordion! It was rescued and returned to its rightful owner, who expressed no surprise at the event, saying only that he knew that he had left it somewhere, and had been certain that someone would return it!

On another occasion, James had bought a very expensive car, and it was only a few weeks old when a friend asked me if I had seen the damage around the boot lock on this beautiful vehicle. I hadn't, but soon afterwards James himself appeared, so we asked what had happened.

'Well, me old fruits,' he explained, 'I was out for the night, and invited some skippers home for a dram. When we got there I couldn't get the boot open to get at the 'carry-out', so I had to take a pick to it, otherwise we'd all have gone thirsty!'

One Hallowe'en he was, thankfully, in a much less expensive car which went off the road. Draped in a white sheet which had peepholes cut into it, he had been making his ghostly visitations to a friend in Morar, about three miles from Mallaig. Whilst negotiating one of the many bends in the road on his return home, the sheet which he was still wearing, slipped around his head. This meant that his eyes were no longer aligned with the holes, and the resultant loss of vision sent the car off the road! This behaviour, which to the less understanding reader might seem crazy, was perhaps not condoned but was almost certainly accepted as necessary by his long-suffering wife, who I am sure knew better than any just how much stress his job could generate. It was certainly understood by me.

A telephone was certainly the most important piece of equipment that a buyer could have in the boom days of the herring fishing, and we were very lucky that we had a team of telephonists in Mallaig who understood how important it was to get through as quickly as possible to the processors we served. To make a call, you simply lifted the telephone, waited until one of the girls answered, and then told her the number you required. This seemingly antiquated technology had advantages which are not readily obvious to anyone who has not used it. More often than not, you simply asked for the required person by name. It was not necessary to remember all the numbers; the girls willingly did it for you. It was common, too, for an incoming call to be diverted to the place where, perhaps, the operator knew you were more likely to be found; or, if she couldn't find you, she would call around all the likely places until she was successful! Eventually, however, progress took the place of common sense. New machinery was installed, and our girls – often referred to by us, with affection, as our call-girls – were made redundant.

One night, just before they all left, they had a going away party in the Exchange, which was going full blast when our James passed on his way home from a ceilidh in the Clachan Bar. He had with him a man who was through from the East Coast on business, a man who lacked the sense to know that he should not try to keep up with James on the drinking scene, and who was now 'carrying more canvas than keel.'

'Ah,' said James, when he heard the noise coming from the exchange, 'the call-girls are having a wee party; we'd better see how it is going, me old fruit.' In went the happy pair, and all went well until our inebriated East Coast friend – having scanned what he thought was on offer – invited one of the perfectly respectable girls to go upstairs with him, proffering a handful of notes as he did so. Not knowing of James's remark to the poor chap on the way in, she took umbrage at this, and threw the foolish fellow out on his neck!

I think we might do a lot worse than to make room for James – and his accordion – at Angus's fireside.

There were almost as many characters on the processing side of the industry, as there were on the catching side. I was privileged to have close dealings with one of the more notable of these characters, Sans Unkles – another certainty for Captaincy.

Sans was a very powerfully built young man who had been a keen rugby player until a bad neck injury put paid to that side of his life. He became the biggest processor of queen scallops in Scotland, working from his factory in Glasgow, and then made what was, with hindsight, the mistake of becoming involved in exporting herring. He rapidly expanded this venture until he was one of the biggest in that scene. I was concerned that he was putting too much faith in the herring boom – which could not, in my opinion, possibly continue – so I took myself to Glasgow to see if I could talk him into slimming down his operation somewhat.

When I arrived, he told Ross Osborne, his financial director, to take me to see his latest factory at Bellshill. The existence of this place was a revelation to me, and news which filled me with foreboding. I could not see how he could continue to get the raw material to keep his existing operation going – to increase the processing capacity was nothing short of lunacy. I was completely mortified when I was told that, in fact, the new place was to be used for processing mackerel! Where on earth was he going to get all the mackerel, I wondered? I felt there were not enough mackerel landed in Scotland in a *year* to keep this factory going for a single *day*.

Everyone now knows that he was correct. A total ban was introduced on herring landings, and history tells us that the pursers found shoals of mackerel in undreamed-of quantities. Sans, however, had acted just six months too early. The financial strain of this new undertaking was too much, the bank pulled the plug on him, and the fishing industry lost the most far-sighted man it had possessed in years. Strange organisations, banks! They call to mind a business which will loan out umbrellas on bonny days, but as soon as they see a cloud on the horizon, they want them back again!

Sans played as hard as he worked, and I have always regretted not accepting an invitation to attend a Hallowe'en party in his house on the southern outskirts of Glasgow. This magnificent house was very old, and had been bought by him as a virtual ruin. Maggie, his beautiful wife, told me that when she first saw inside it – prior to it being renovated – she sat down in the hall and cried, because she could see the sky through the roof! Some of the events of the night of the party were told to me later.

A bus had been organised to pick up the guests in town and take them to the house, and later to take them home at the end of the night. This arrangement solved two potential problems: firstly, no one had to worry about drinking and driving; and, just as importantly, everyone left at the same time!

Sans had hired a piper, clad in full Highland dress, to welcome the guisers when they arrived. As soon as the bus was in sight, Sans ushered the musician up a ladder to the battlements so that he could stand on them to play. He then removed the ladder, so not to spoil the splendid visual effect of this magnificently clad piper, who was, of course, illuminated by a floodlight.

The guests, all in fancy dress, were ushered into the house amidst great jollification, the door was closed, and the outside lights switched off. Some considerable time had passed before someone fortunately heard the plaintive calls for help which emanated from the poor, completely frozen, piper who had been stranded on the roof!

I was reliably told of Sans's first connection with Highland cattle, which he loved, and which grazed the grounds around this house. He had been at a cattle auction in Oban one day, with a pal, and had wakened up the following morning, not only with a hangover but also as the proud but puzzled owner of a Highland cow! It was in calf, and in due course the birth was announced in the *Glasgow Herald* – 'To Bella, a son Rory. Both well'!

He was the biggest independent shellfish producer in the UK at a very early

97

age indeed, and was also the first in the country to have a shrimp-shucking machine, an achievement which he likened to being a pheasant plucker to trade!

The final man in this sphere to be invited to Angus's fireside is James Burgon of Eyemouth. A big man, who became very stout in his later years, he was a lobster, crab, herring, and whitefish-processor. It is generally agreed among all who were privileged to have known him, that he was one of the most honest and upright men ever to have taken part in the fishing industry, and I certainly consider it an honour to have known, and to have dealt with him.

I remember taking him to task on one occasion early in our dealings together. When a lorry load of herring was despatched, the driver was always given a delivery line which would simply read, for example '100 crans herring @ £15'. This was purely a delivery line, and was not an account. James paid on this line, which meant him issuing perhaps ten cheques to me in a week, and also meant difficulties for me when I tried to reconcile, with the account sent out to him at the end of the week, what he had already paid. James's reply was that his last action every day of business was to sign and send out cheques for all that he had received that day. It had always been thus, and he was not going to change it for me! I wonder what he would think of business practice today, which seems to dictate that firms hold on to monies owed to others for as long as is possible.

He told me one day that he had once had a dispute with the skipper of a boat, and that this man had, in a temper, told James that he would never sell him anything else again for as long as he lived. I never forgot the reply:

'Well,' said James, 'I am fifty-four years old now, and for fifty-three of these years I never knew that you existed. I got on fine without you, and I am sure that I'll continue that way if I never hear of you again!'

Billy Buchan, one of his trusted managers and a shareholder in the firm, told me that one day, many years ago, James took some fifty boxes of haddock from a boat who just could not sell them, gave the owner £5 a box for them, and told Billy to send them to Granton Market. Two days later, he sent for the skipper of this boat, and proffered an envelope of cash.

'What's this for?' queried the man.

'It's the balance of what I owe you for those haddock. You see, I got more for them than I expected,' replied James.

I may be cynical, but I just cannot see this happening now – anywhere. In his fish processing yard could be found old men who had worked for James, or for his father John, all their lives. When it came time for workers to retire, or if through illness they became unfit for heavy work, they all knew that some kind of job would be found for them at the yard, among the men with whom they had toiled for so long.

10

There were of course several men in and around Mallaig who were not directly connected with the fishing industry, but who would certainly qualify as Captains, and who would be welcome at many a fireside apart from Angus's.

Foremost of these in my opinion has got to be Charlie Henderson, who although now officially retired, still works in the boatyard in Mallaig which he owned and ran successfully all his working life. He also served with distinction as Coxswain of the local Lifeboat for many years. Sparsely built, and of medium height, he has a disconcertingly quizzical way of looking at the person he is addressing. He is very well known and respected in many places.

I was aboard the Lifeboat with him on one occasion when we called at Tobermory to get something to eat, hungry after a particularly long service. We went into the Mishnish Hotel, to be told by the young receptionist that we were too late for lunch and too early for dinner; but we agreed to wait till she could get some sandwiches made up for us. While we waited, Bobby MacLeod the owner appeared, and hailed our hero like a long-lost brother.

'What brings you here, Charlie?' he asked. When Charlie told him we were waiting for sandwiches to be made up, Bobby's roars had to be heard to be believed. An hour later we sat down to a sumptuous feast in the dining room of the Mishnish. On our way out, having been subjected first of all to a real West Highland row for daring to attempt to pay for the meal, we were given the sandwiches 'in case you get hungry on the way home!'

Whilst writing of the Lifeboat, I am reminded of a story told to me as true recently, by one of the fund-raising staff of the Royal National Lifeboat Institution.

He had gone one morning to visit a man who had been of great help to the RNLI in the past. When he arrived at what could best be described as 'The Manor', which was situated in its own estate somewhere in central Scotland, he was taken into the kitchen, where his host made tea for them both. As they sat there discussing their business, the aged mother of the host came tottering into the kitchen, made a beeline for a cabinet which stood in a corner and, opening the door of this cabinet, poured and downed a glassful of some amber liquid, then tottered out again without a word being spoken.

Ten minutes later this process was repeated, but this time the son exclaimed: 'Mother!! That's your second, and it is only ten o'clock in the morning.'

The old dear turned round and replied in her beautiful aristocratic accent, 'Would you have me walk around on one leg all day then?'

As she turned round to make this statement, my informant noticed that the bottle from which she had poured her drink was clearly labelled 'Parazone', in large red felt-tip letters. Seeing his horrified look, she nonchalantly offered by way of explanation: 'Take no heed of this. I put that label on to keep my housekeeper away from it. She's an alcoholic, don't you see!'

Another of my Captains arrived in Mallaig shortly before I left, and has since then died suddenly at a very young age. I first met Father John MacNeill when he was the priest at Inverie in Knoydart. He was sent from there to Eriskay, where he tended to the needs of his flock for a few years before being posted to Fort William, becoming a Canon. Eventually he got the posting to Morar which was, I think, his greatest desire, although he sadly did not get very long to enjoy it. Brought up in a seafaring community in Barra, he loved nothing more than to be in the company of fishermen.

It would be fair to say that, whilst he was at Inverie, he developed the habit of drinking far too much for his own good, a habit which followed him to Eriskay. I therefore assumed that he was still fond of a dram when he arrived at Morar, so when he visited us one day in Mallaig, I offered him one, which to my surprise he refused. When I asked if he had stopped drinking, he told me that he still took a little wine or, if he was feeling cold on arriving home late on a winter evening, he would have a brandy. He then told me a remarkable story which I will repeat, changing it only slightly to protect the feelings of a few friends.

In another parish, he told me, he had become concerned for the well-being of the marriage of two of his parishioners, and it came as no shock to him when the wife telephoned him late one evening, and asked for his counsel. He told her to come round right away, with her husband, and when they were all seated around the table, Father John poured a large glass of sherry for the wife, and produced a bottle of whisky and glasses for him and the man.

It took a long time for them to drag the root of the problem into the open, but eventually all agreed that too much drinking was the prime cause. This accomplished, Father John filled the last remaining drams from the bottle and challenged the husband:

'I will toast you with this dram on the condition that we toast one another with the next dram we take.'

In other words he was saying that he would stop if the man before him would do the same. This agreed, they downed the drinks, and the couple went home.

'This took place just before Christmas,' Canon John told me, 'and I watched and worried all the time, especially over the New Year period, but he never put a foot wrong. He went back to sea shortly after the Festive time was finished, and was lost overboard one dark night, so you see, I won't take a dram until he is there for me to toast with it!'

I do not share Canon MacNeill's faith, but his life was an example to me of what religious tolerance really means, and his humanity guarantees him as good a reception at Angus's fireside as he ever got from his many friends in this life.

His predecessor was Canon Macinnes, who was also well-loved in the area, and who was the prime mover in a hilarious incident which would not be out of place in one of the many tales about Para Handy. This concerned a scattering of ashes on Loch Morar. These ashes were of a man known to me only as Watty, a very gentle man who had moved to the area from around Glasgow, and whose love of

Loch Morar eventually led to his death by drowning in it. His body was cremated, and the Canon decided that the ashes should be scattered on the waters which he had loved so much.

(The story of this ceremony involves several other characters who must be introduced to the reader who is not fortunate enough to know them personally.)

Donny MacLellan is better known as 'Donny-by-gosh', a nickname originating from his habitual response, as a child, to the question 'What's your name?' 'Donny, by gosh' would be the unfailing reply. He owns the boat which was used by the burial party, and his inborn reluctance to waste hard-earned cash on the upkeep of this boat is central to the tale. He is a stocky, well built man – weight is also an important part of this story!

John MacVarish is Donny's bosom pal and constant angling companion. This wiry character was born at the head of Loch Morar, spent his formative years there, and fishes it as often as he can, so his knowledge of the loch in all its moods is unsurpassed. They also on occasion, shared a wee dram together.

Ronnie MacLellan – 'Ronnie Seaview' as he is always called – was recruited by the Canon as official piper for the event, and was instructed to play a lament as the cortege left the river. Ronnie is as heavily built as the Canon.

The day dawned and Donny and John, having spent some time in the bar of Morar Hotel putting the finishing touches to the plans for the day, went down to the river. There they saw the Canon, who was in his eighties, and Ronnie Seaview safely aboard the boat, and set off out of the river at the head of a convoy, which bore all who had come to pay their last respects. Ronnie struck up his lament, and John – under instruction from the Canon – held fast to the casket of ashes which, on the word of command from the Canon, he was to scatter reverently on the waters.

Several years earlier, Donny had noticed that his boat had a slight leak, and had intended repairing this minor defect whenever he could borrow a little drop of the necessary fibreglass repair compound from someone. Now, on the way out of the river, he realised that the extra weight of the burial party was causing the boat to sit lower in the water, and that the leak – previously a trickle – was now becoming somewhat more serious. His reaction to this was similar to that of any true Highland gentleman – ignore it and hope that it goes away! And so he became very interested in the cloud formations, studiously ignoring the furtive but frantic attempts of John to bring the rapidly increasing flood to his attention!

John, failing to get Donnie's attention, concentrated his thoughts on whether or not the casket was buoyant enough to keep him afloat, and was measuring the relative distances between the shore and the nearest boat in the cortege.

The Canon had his eyes closed, thinking no doubt on higher things, and was oblivious to the waters gathering around his feet. Ronnie's attention was only drawn to this life-threatening phenomenon when his foot, previously tapping in time to the music, started splashing instead!

Water running over the top of the Canon's ankle boot finally brought to him the realisation of *why* Ronnie's pibroch was now being played at jig time, and a frantic nudge brought immediate silence from the relieved Ronnie, and he quickly launched into the short service.

The Beach at Mallaig Harbour
(Susan Hughan)

'In the name of the Father, Son...' This was blurted out at great speed, and John, whose reactions were by now honed to razor sharpness, threw the ashes instinctively... to windward, scattering them over the attendant congregation rather than over Watty's beloved Loch Morar. I am certain that Watty was rolling around laughing somewhere.

Donnie some time ago surprised everyone by taking his wife on a holiday to the West Indies. I met him when he returned and, knowing that this was generally felt to be an expensive part of the world in which to holiday, I asked him what the cost of living was like there. He showed that he had his priorities right when he replied after due consideration, 'Well, rum is cheap, but whisky is a hellova price!'

The possibility of Willie Kirk being promoted to Captain may well surprise many people but, remember, these are *my* Captains.

Willie comes from a family with strong Mallaig connections, and he first came to my notice when he returned from a long sojourn in America, to assist his uncle in the running of the grocery and hardware shop at the head of the pier in Mallaig. He presents an unkempt, kenspeckle figure, and to those who do not know him, his shyness and very slow speech suggests that he is inward-looking, and rather forbidding. His balding pate is usually fringed by long strands of fair hair, but on the rare occasion when Willie dresses up, the transformation to the epitome of a smart business man is completed by the brushing of this hair over the bald patches, and has to be seen to be believed.

His stay in America was mainly in San Francisco, where he worked with another uncle who owned a bar there called *The Edinburgh Castle*. My first real meeting with him was when I casually mentioned to him that my wife and I were shortly going to visit San Francisco, whereupon Willie produced a scrap piece of paper and drew, purely from memory, a map of the city including street names and numbers, indicating on it just where his uncle's pub was to be found. When we arrived, I found the scrap of paper to be so amazingly accurate that I used it to find my way around! I have since become convinced that Willie's idiosyncrasy is a deliberate cover for a very highly intelligent man, a conviction which is shared by many who have come to know him better than I.

He had not long arrived in Mallaig when I discovered the joys of fishing on Loch Morar, a fresh water loch famed for being the deepest freshwater loch in Europe, and which is joined to the sea by what is reputed to be the shortest river in the UK. Fishing there consisted mainly of trolling, towing various sizes and colours of lures behind one's boat, in the fond and often futile hope that a trout, or even a salmon, might find it attractive. Willie's Uncle Bertie, who owned the shop where Willie worked, sold rods and lures, and he had himself fished the loch for many years, so I allowed myself to be guided by him in my choice of gear. Now, I did not expect to become an expert at once, but I was certainly not prepared to accept that for every trout *I* caught, others caught six or eight, so I pestered the life out of poor Bertie, telling him that this failure of mine must be directly attributable to the poor quality of the lures he sold!

103

One day, having been fishing for about three hours with a total lack of success, I came into the river on Morar where we kept our boats to find another fisherman – who had berthed just before me – standing on the road. Noticing that he did not have his car there, I offered him a lift into Mallaig, which he refused, saying that he was just in to collect his son who had been working, and intended going back out onto the loch again. He asked me if I had caught anything, and when I replied in the negative, he completed my discomfiture by saying that he had about a dozen trout. However, when I jokingly asked him for a couple for my tea, he refused.

Smelling a rat, I offered Jackie a fiver for one trout. His refusal confirmed the suspicion which had been slowly dawning on me. He had none! The enormous relief at finding out that my lowly position in the catching stakes was due to the fact that the others were telling lies, was something to relish. My first call in Mallaig was at Bertie's shop, where I wanted to tell him of my new-found knowledge, but instead I found Willie there alone.

'Aye,' he said, when I had blurted out my tale. 'Tell me, do you subscribe to the Monte Carlo theory?'

Seeing my puzzled look, he continued in his usual slow drawl: 'Aye, the Monte Carlo theory is that, if you toss a coin ten times, and it comes down heads every time, then it is odds on that it'll fall heads on the eleventh time too.' Pausing for a moment to allow me to digest this offering, he slowly resumed. 'The anti-Monte Carlo theory, however, is that having come down heads ten times, it is odds on that it will change – so it will be tails the eleventh time.'

'What has this got to do with fishing on the loch?' I questioned him.

'Aye,' said Willie at his usual slow pace, 'I was just coming to that. You see, one man catches a trout in bay X on Morar, and when you meet him and see this braw fish, you ask him where he got it, he'll tell you it was in bay Y, because he thinks that bay X is a good place for trout, and he wants to keep it for himself.'

'Now another man catches a trout in bay A on the loch, but he thinks that he has chased all the trout out of that bay, so when you ask him where he caught it, he'll tell you correctly that he got it in bay A, for he is sure that there are no more left there.'

By now I was completely flummoxed, so Willie, sensing this, said, 'Do you not see what I mean?'

'No,' was the best I could muster.

'Aye, well it's easy. I'm just trying to say that you canna believe a bloody word anyone tells you!'

Willie is fond of playing bridge, and is one of a group which still plays every week at a friend's house. Some years ago they had gathered for their game, but before it started, the conversation turned to a topic which was currently headline news – as it still so often sadly is – a sex attack on a young girl. They were all vociferous in their condemnation of this revolting crime, and were discussing the various punishments which should be dished out to the perpetrator when, during a lull, Willie announced that he personally had once attempted to have sex with an eight-year old girl. There was stunned silence, and then one of the ladies present turned her full armament on him, sparing nothing in her attack. Willie eventually managed to stem the flow of vituperation, and quietly said, 'Wait a minute, Molly. I was only six-years old myself at the time!'

Some time ago, Willie became a member of the local Community Council. One night, the meeting of Council was dominated by certain members bewailing the dearth of tourists in the season just past, which had cut their income drastically. Various suggestions were being put forward as possibly being of help in promoting the natural attractions of the area, and it was generally agreed that more publicity should be sought. Willie had taken no active part in the discussion, but then he got the natural pause for which he had been waiting.

'Aye, we'll buy some baby palm trees,' he announced.

Silence continued, while the others attempted to make sense of this mouthful.

'Aye, we'll need to get the Roads Department to agree to their workmen planting the trees; and we'll wait until we get a good long spell of really hard frost – you know the kind of weather I mean, when the transport system has collapsed, the roads are icy, and the signals and points are all frozen on the railway. Permafrost three feet deep in the ground. Aye. Then we'll tell the roadmen to plant the trees. They'll refuse of course, saying that it is crazy to try to plant any kind of trees, never mind palm trees, in this kind of weather. We'll make an issue of it, and insist that they do it right away, so they'll go on strike. This strike will spread all over the country, and of course will make national news. People shivering all over Britain will see this, and they are bound to say "What kind of place is this that can plant palm trees while we are all in the grip of a freeze?" – and just you wait and see, they'll flock here in their thousands next year!'

Willie carried his lack of urgency into his shop, where he was happy to chat to a customer after a sale, completely ignoring the growing queue of increasingly impatient people waiting for him to attend to them. One day, a colleague of mine, who was not renowned for his patience, went in to see if Willie stocked any of the patent cat deterrents with which he hoped to rid himself of a growing nuisance of stray cats in his garden. He found Willie, head down in a tea chest full of new stock for the hardware department, busily unpacking and checking the contents. Having been studiously ignored for about five minutes, he blurted out impatiently, 'Willie, have you anything to chase cats away?' Without even looking up, Willie in his usual slow drawl replied, 'Aye, have you tried a dog?'

One great regret concerning Willie is that I was not present in Colin Thom's house one evening when Willie performed The Dance of the Dying Swan to the music of *Swan Lake*, dressed in a pair of pink tights belonging to Colin's daughter!

Yes, indeed, Willie would fit in very well with the Captains by the fireside.

My final Captain is the only one who really did wear the four gold rings of Captain on his sleeves. He was skipper of the famous original *LochMor*, one of David MacBrayne's steamers. Captain Robertson was a short, stocky man with a ruddy seaman's complexion, who spoke in a very high-pitched voice. This led to his being better known as 'Squeaky' Robertson.

I first encountered Squeaky in the bar of the Imperial Hotel in Fort William many years ago, when he was entertaining four English gentlemen, who were in turn buying him whisky. I was waiting for the train to Mallaig, and had bought a book to help pass the time away, but I'm afraid that I did precious little reading, becoming as engrossed as his friends were in the tales he had to tell. He was a born storyteller, and once again, it is a great pity that no one had the foresight to record these tales of his for posterity.

I have heard many times of the occasion when he was caught in a severe gale on passage from Mallaig to Lochboisdale in South Uist. They had an extremely bad passage across the wild waters of the Minch on the dark winter's night, and great was the relief of all aboard when at last they reached the safety of the pier. As soon as the ship was safely tied up, Squeaky took his place as usual at the head of the gangplank to see his passengers ashore, but on this occasion two dear old ladies, who had suffered badly from seasickness and from fear on the passage, grasped his hands and with great emotion exclaimed: 'That was a dreadful night Captain. We know that our safe arrival is due to the grace of God and to your skill!'

'Aye, aye' was the instant reply from Squeaky. 'Two good men!'

On a similarly wild day, Captain Robertson decided to delay the departure from Lochboisdale until the weather had eased a bit, and had related his decision to the passengers. One lady, who for reasons of her own was very keen to be away, on hearing this, disputed that the weather was that bad, and indignantly pointed out a blue patch in the sky to Squeaky to strengthen her argument.

'Aye, aye madam, but we're not going up there though, we're going to Mallaig,' was the reply!

Another oft-related tale also concerned two genteel old ladies, though not the same pair as in the previous tale. This time the duo had booked a passage on a trip which took them around Skye, and as one of them had some clout with MacBraynes, Captain Robertson had been instructed by his seniors in Glasgow to afford them every courtesy, including allowing them free access to the bridge – which went sore against the grain with him. Just south of Dunvegan on the west coast of Skye stands 'MacLeod's Maidens', three most impressive pillars of rock similar to the Old Man of Hoy, jutting vertically from the sea below the very high cliffs. The old dears were on the bridge as the *LochMor* passed this landmark, and one of them asked if it had a name. 'They are called MacLeod's Maidens', was the reply from Squeaky, who was by now thoroughly fed up with the pair's continuing presence on the bridge of his ship.

'Is there a story behind this name, Captain?,' was the next question from one of the ladies, who hoped no doubt to be regaled with some gem of historical allusion like the tale of Lot's wife.

'Well, yes, madam. You see, there has never been a man on top of them!'

A veil has rightly been drawn over the response from the 'Head Office', when this remark was later related to them by the indignant ladies.

Archie MacLellan told me that when his father, also named Archie, built the Clachain Bar, opened in 1939 after war had started, one of the immediate problems confronting him was the introduction of a whisky ration which was based upon the previous year's consumption which was, of course, in his case – nil! The problem was overcome with the help of the Gaelic-speaking head of a whisky-blending and bottling company in Glasgow, who hailed originally from Skye, and who had known old Archie in his younger days. The connection re-established, the Skye man then over a period of years sent several bottles of whisky to Mallaig at Christmas time, with a note of the people to whom old Archie had to present them. Squeaky always benefited to the tune of two bottles of what, in the war years, was liquid gold, but one year his name was not on the list. This omission greatly surprised Archie, and he was faced with the diplomatically difficult decision of whether or not he should bring this state of affairs to the attention of the benefactor.

Eventually, however, he telephoned Glasgow on another pretext, and spoke to the gentleman himself. Pleasantries concluded, he brought up the case of the missing bottles. All was revealed in the story which followed.

Squeaky, he was told, had arrived in the blender's office in person just a week or so previously. He sat down and made himself at home, having placed at his feet a small case. The yarns showed no sign of abating and eventually, in order to get on with his work, the now reluctant host suggested that he give Squeaky the whisky in person, thinking that he might then be left in peace.

This of course met with instant approval, and a girl was despatched to fetch two bottles of the best. When she returned and handed them to our Captain, he promptly retrieved the case from the floor, opened it (in so doing revealing that it was completely empty), and put the two bottles into it. He then quizzically regarded the still open case quietly for a few moments and eventually remarked thoughtfully – almost speaking to himself – 'If I only had a half bottle to jam between them, it would keep them from rattling together!'

Squeaky, then, completes the list of guests which I have presumed to invite to share a dram by Angus's fireside. Too often our forgiving human nature dictates to us that 'late' is synonymous with 'great'. I have tried to resist this failing, if indeed it is a failing. Not that all of the people I have nominated as Captains are 'late' – fortunately many are still with us. If I have conveyed to you, the reader, just a fraction of the joy I have had in recalling my memories of these men who were giants to me, then perhaps this sharing will help to ensure that they will not be forgotten.

SMH '85